KV-057-392

# Black Hearts
# Black Spades

Orphaned after tragic events during a dreadful storm, two young children, Jacob and Rachel Peterson, leave Beckinson in the foothills of the Rocky Mountains for adoption by an uncle and aunt in Chicago. Ten years later, when the opportunity arises to expand his uncle's business, Jacob chooses to set up in Beckinson. Fifteen-year-old Rachel remembers nothing of the past and is unaware of the anger that is consuming her brother. Jacob is set on discovering the truth behind the events that took their parents, but Beckinson is now rife with corruption: a degenerate and dangerous town where outlaws walk free. What could Jacob possibly do against that?

*By the same author*

The Danville Stagecoach Robbery

# Black Hearts Black Spades

Frank Chandler

**A Black Horse Western**

ROBERT HALE

© Frank Chandler 2017
First published in Great Britain 2017

ISBN 978-0-7198-2245-2

The Crowood Press
The Stable Block
Crowood Lane
Ramsbury
Marlborough
Wiltshire SN8 2HR

www.bhwesterns.com

Robert Hale is an imprint
of The Crowood Press

The right of Frank Chandler to be identified as
author of this work has been asserted by him
in accordance with the Copyright, Designs and
Patents Act 1988

Typeset by
Derek Doyle & Associates, Shaw Heath
Printed and bound in Great Britain by
CPI Group (UK) Ltd, Croydon, CR0 4YY

# 1

The two children slid down under the covers as rain hit the windowpanes like dried peas thrown against a wall. Gusts of wind howled eerily round the gables, searching endlessly for the slightest of gaps. Jacob's little sister, Rachel, had rolled right across the bed at the first rumble of the storm, and clung to him as if her life depended on it. The night was as black as it could possibly be and Jacob was wanting to call out to his parents for reassurance. He was torn between the need for an adult, and the desire to be done with childish fear. He had to protect his sister, but needed some comfort himself. Weren't his ten years a good enough age to become a man? Ten is a fine age to be when everything is going well. Right now Jacob struggled, but bit his lip and kept his silence. He told himself there are times to act older than you are, especially when you have responsibility for someone younger and more helpless than yourself. He sounded like his father and that filled him with pride. Rachel was just half his age and Jacob would always be strong for her.

The wind picked up and rain lashed the ranch house in a deluge of fury. Jacob whispered in Rachel's ear: 'Sis, can you remember how to say the Lord's prayer?'

'Sure,' she replied.

'Go on then, you start it,' he said, not because he had

forgotten, but he thought it would give her something more comforting to concentrate on than the howling gale and gripping his ribs quite so tightly.

'Our Father—'

'Sssh.'

Jacob clamped his hand over her mouth and silenced her before she had hardly begun. It sounded like someone was knocking at the ranch-house door. His parents were in the main room chatting together by the fireside. Their quiet conversation suddenly stopped too. The knocking was louder. 'Rebecca, put some coffee on,' Jacob's father said, 'it sounds like we've got some storm-weary travellers.'

'Are you going to let them in, Zachary?' she replied. 'At this time of night?'

Zachary was already out of his chair and opening the door to the travellers. Were they lost in the storm? The ranch was only a few miles out of town but in this weather you could lose your way even on a path you were familiar with.

Jacob strained his ears. He eased himself out of Rachel's grip and left his sister snuggled down under the covers. He crept out of bed. There was a tiny hole near the bedroom door where a knot had come out of the pine boarding and he often used it to hear what was going on in the main room. It was low and awkward and because of the thickness of the board he couldn't see much of the room, but he could usually hear all of the talking.

The ranch door was opened and the storm blew some people into the house. It sounded like three riders with jingling spurs, strangers perhaps caught in the storm. No, not strangers after all; his father knew them, they were talking, saying hello and that sort of thing. Ambrose, Clem and Tod had come on a visit. Wet slickers were being taken off and hung up, one of the men came partly into sight; it looked like he was wearing a gunbelt. Jacob's pa didn't usually like people carrying guns inside the house.

The visitors had brought some whiskey and were offering his pa a drink. Glasses chinked on the sideboard. Jacob had never seen his pa drinking whiskey at home. His ma offered them some cheese and bread. She said she was just making some coffee, but they insisted on glasses of whiskey. They were all just out of Jacob's sight. Sitting close to the fire the visitors were drying out, just one voice was talking. A deep sonorous voice, calm, slow, unpleasant. Why unpleasant? There was something about the delivery of the words. It wasn't calm like in a relaxed conversation, it was calm because there was a hint of menace. Jacob put his ear to the hole to listen more carefully. He heard his pa speak.

'Why in tarnation have you come out here on a night like this, and at this hour?'

'See sense, Zachary. I'm offering to give you a good deal, but my patience is wearing real thin.'

'I ain't selling, Ambrose, you know that. I wasn't before, and I ain't now. We've built this land up good and the beeves are doin' good too. There's plenty land all round to the east if you want more; why keep pestering us? What's so special about these acres of grass?'

'It ain't the grass I'm after. Now drink up, Zachary. Tod, give him another glass.'

'I don't want any more of your whiskey, Ambrose. Now I'd really like you to leave before— '

'I ain't leaving, Zachary, until you agree to sell. I've spoke reason with you enough times. Clem's got the papers right here and you're going to sign them now.'

There was a pause but no response from Jacob's pa. The man called Ambrose, who was obviously in charge, spoke again.

'Tod, Clem, hold him down.'

Jacob couldn't see what was happening but there was the sound of a struggle.

His ma's voice was shrill.

'Ambrose, leave him alone!'

'Shut up, bitch!' There was a slap and Jacob heard his ma cry out in pain. Ambrose continued:

'Clem, open his mouth and pour it down his throat.'

Another pause in the conversation; Jacob could hear his pa spluttering and choking. The man his pa had called Ambrose spoke again.

'It ain't no use shakin' yer head at me, Zachary Peterson. I want this land and you will sign. Make him see sense, Rebecca. Our only decent access to the mine is across this land, and I'm givin' a fair price.'

'Ambrose, you can't have everything you want,' Jacob's ma pleaded. 'Zachary ain't never goin' to sell. This is our life's work, it's all we've got for our children and you aren't going to take it from us.' A cupboard door opened, there was a sound of steel blades. 'Get out now!'

It sounded like his ma had probably got a couple of skinning knives. But there was another slap, a dull thud, knives clattering and his pa was still choking and spluttering.

'I've gone beyond askin' you to sell. Now I'm just askin' you to sign. You had the chance for a fair price. You refused, so now I'll just take it with a signature.'

Rachel had got out of bed and was tugging at Jacob's nightshirt. He grabbed her and pressed her head into his side, so she couldn't hear the commotion. Jacob was rooted to the spot, gripped by the childish fear that he had been hoping to conquer. He could hear his pa trying to speak but the words were all blurred and spluttery. There was a kind of tense calm in the room, but Jacob could hear his ma sobbing.

The deep voice tried to sound reassuring but the menace remained.

'You see, Rebecca; I told you he was no good for you.

You've lost everything now. You should have married me when you had the chance. Now look at you. Your dress is ripped, your lip's bleeding. You're not a pretty sight, Rebecca. What do you think, Zachary? Is she a good wife?'

There was a muffled, slurred kind of response which was just a noise without words. One of the other men spoke.

'Come on, Ambrose, we're done here. Zachary's got the message. He couldn't hold a pen now anyway. His eyes are rollin' all over the place. There ain't no use doin' any more. We can come back in the morning.'

'Keep out of it, Tod. I didn't come here just for the paperwork. I came here for the woman as well – and I'm going to have her. Put a gag in her mouth.'

'Ambrose—'

'Do it!'

Jacob heard a gun being pulled out of a holster and the unmistakable click of the firing pin being cocked. Ambrose's deep voice was unhurried, savouring every word and what they were leading to.

'You can go if you want, Tod. Clem, you too, but I ain't finished yet.'

Suddenly there was a flurry of fighting and screaming; his ma was being gagged and she was kicking out by the sound of it. There was punching and yelling, ripping of material, then everything went quiet again.

'See, Zachary, she was trying to stop me. She really was. But look at her now, with Clem holding her at the ready. Saints alive! Ain't she a pretty one without her dress, and those natty white drawers on the floor? I expect you'd like to shoot me, Zachary, wouldn't you?'

'Sonofa, son – son – sonofa. . . .' His pa sounded half-asleep: what was he doing? Jacob couldn't understand why his pa wasn't doing anything to protect Rebecca, his ma. Ambrose spoke again.

'Here, Zachary, take this gun and shoot me.'

There was a scrabbling of struggle followed by a deafening shot and a piercing scream.

'Jesus, Ambrose, the bastard's shot me! Why did you give him the gun to wave about like that?'

'It's a flesh wound Tod; shut yer noise up.' Ambrose was laughing. 'Oh dear, Zachary, was that shot meant for me? You ain't seeing too good, are you? Now look what you've done, gone and shot Tod!'

Now, for the first time, Jacob saw the man called Tod as he fell on the floor near the knothole, his hand pressed to his thigh and a look of uncomprehending shock on his face. Another man – it must have been the one called Clem – came over and knelt down beside Tod.

'Don't worry, brother, you ain't going to die from that.'

'It would suit you if I did, wouldn't it? Tod struggled to get the words out. 'Devil's Leap would be yours. Sure you didn't arrange this?'

'Now, brother, why would I do that? Zachary's too drunk to aim the gun; he just fired a wild shot. Ambrose has taken the gun away.'

'You want the silver mine all to yourself, don't you, Clem?' Tod's breathing was heavy and forced. 'You always were a grabbing bastard, never shared a damn thing as a kid, did you? My little baby brother who wanted everything for himself. Now you can't stomach sharing the mine. Our pa knew it would provide more than enough for both of us when he filed the claim.'

'God rest his soul,' said Clem. 'But he forgot about an access road.'

Tod's face screwed up again. 'Jesus, my leg hurts! But sharing ain't in your nature, is it?'

'No.'

What happened next was so shocking that Jacob wasn't sure if it really did happen. Tod's face contorted again with pain. Clem stood up and walked away but there was another sudden deafening blast as a shot hit Tod full in the chest, killing him instantly. Jacob felt the vibration in the floorboards. 'That's done,' said Ambrose.

'God forgive us,' said Clem. 'So, big brother, that's what yer get for all the years of pokin' fun at me. Now I get Devil's Leap all to myself.'

'Well, not quite, Clem,' Ambrose said. 'You see, I told you it'd turn out right. I'll give you access across Zachary's land for a share of the mine profits. Then we can grow the town and make ourselves real important people. Now come over here and hold this woman steady.'

The gagged and muffled screams would ring for ever in Jacob's ears. There was more slapping, punching, struggling. Then everything went quiet.

'Well, Zachary, my old buddie, that's a mighty fine woman you've got. Look at him, Clem, he's out cold. Put the gun in his hand and fix it good. We're nearly done here. Just got to deal with those two kids of theirs.'

# 2

Suddenly all the heavy chains that had held Jacob trans-
fixed to the spot were thrown off. Now there was only one
place that would be safe: an outbuilding. Having been built
in the time when Cheyenne Indian raids were not uncom-
mon, there was a hiding place in one of the outbuildings.
Quickly Jacob wrapped Rachel in a blanket, then opened
the window, lifted his five-year-old sister on to the ledge and
dropped her into the pouring rain. He climbed quietly on
to the sill and quickly followed her, pushing the window
shut and dropping silently into the mud.

He scrambled them both into the outbuilding and slid
his hand under the edge of the heavy floor cover. He cut his
finger as, desperately, he fiddled with the rusty catch, but
eventually it was released and they slipped down inside. The
hatch closed. Jacob slid the bolt. They were hidden and safe
in the underground refuge. The stowed blankets smelled
musty, but welcome nonetheless. Rachel was sobbing. Jacob
was traumatized by their dangerous plight, but he managed
to put his arm round Rachel and whisper that everything
would be all right.

It wasn't long before he heard footsteps and voices
swirling with the wind. Jacob prayed that their hiding-place

wouldn't be discovered. His heart was beating out the time in thumping seconds. Now the wind was less violent, but the rain continued thrashing. The sounds of spurs and horse-harness jingled on the wind, then hoofbeats. These visitors hadn't actually stayed very long at the ranch; everything had been done in less than half an hour and now it was eerily quiet. Straining above the throbbing noise in his ears, all Jacob could hear was the muffled drumming of rainfall on the timber roof. Exhausted by his outflow of nervous energy, his head gradually slumped forward until it reached his chest.

Jacob woke with a start. Was it morning? How long had he slept? He squeezed open a gap and weak daylight infiltrated the hiding place. He realized the sun must be up. Its rays were pushing through the gaps in the shed wall. Rachel was still fast asleep but now they must move and find out what had happened. Were there still any bad people at the ranch? Where were his ma and pa, and was it safe to go out? He undid the catch quietly and peered out.

The ranch was totally quiet. The air was tinged with the smell of fresh rain and wet mud. Surely his pa's regular ranch hand, John, who lived in the town, should be out here by now? Jacob eased himself out of the hole and, still in his nightshirt and without any shoes, he stepped through the puddles round to the ranch door and went in. There was blood on the table, blood on the floor, a massive dark-red pool and smears where the man called Tod had been shot in the chest and dragged away. A long sharp skinning-knife lay on the floor by the kitchen table. There were other things that he noticed but didn't want to see.

'Jacob?'

He swung round, startled out of his skin. It was John.

'Where's Rachel? God! What a mess. Are you both safe? Listen, you've to gather up some clothes, Jacob, for you and

Rachel. I've got a bag for them, I'm taking the two of you back to my house.'

'Where's my parents?'

'They're in town. Get Rachel and the clothes. Where is she?' John asked.

Jacob was in a daze. John gave him a carpetbag and he collected up some clothes from the wardrobe. They went to the outbuilding and extracted Rachel from the hiding place. Her eyes were still full of sleep and she blinked at the sun. 'Jacob,' she said, 'I'm hungry.'

Jacob saddled his pony and put Rachel up behind. John rode with them into town. As they started down Beckinson's main street people began to gather on the boardwalks. They just stood and stared.

'What are they looking at?' Jacob asked John.

'Just curious, I guess,' he replied.

But it was more than curiosity that drew the townsfolk to stop and stare. There was pity in their eyes and frowns on the faces of some; but the silence was the most strange thing of all. It felt like a funeral.

They hitched up outside John's house. His wife, Abigail, came out to greet them. She wiped the flour off her hands on to her apron and fussed with Rachel, scooping her up and whisking her inside. Jacob turned a puzzled look towards John. John ruffled his hair.

'We'll work something out,' he said.

Rachel didn't understand why she couldn't see her mummy. Jacob tried to explain that their ma was very tired and resting at the doctor's house. She'd be right in a few days and they could go and see her, but just now they had to leave her to sleep and get better.

'Get better?' Rachel queried. 'Is mummy ill?'

'Yes, in a way. Stop asking questions about it, Rachey, and finish your drawing. We'll see her soon enough.'

Jacob knew that his mother had been punched and slapped, he'd heard all that, but he didn't want to say so to Rachel. She didn't need to know, and in truth he didn't understand too much about it himself. John had said the doctor was looking after her; she had to rest and couldn't see any visitors yet. She was probably badly bruised and Jacob didn't want to see her like that anyway.

In fact she had been so badly beaten that her life was in danger.

What Jacob found more difficult to understand was why his pa was in the sheriff's lock-up. He hadn't been allowed to see him, either. John was his only source of information and John simply said his pa was in there for his own good. It was all very baffling for a young lad who was beginning to feel that childish fears of storms in the dark were no big deal compared with his present worries.

That was the morning that Sheriff Hal Hart called round for a chat.

The sheriff sat himself down in the big easy chair in John's living room. John and Abigail sat by the door, and Jacob had to stand in front of the sheriff. He felt nervous and his eyes kept fixing on the pearl-handled six-gun that he could see in the sheriff's holster. There were shiny brass bullet cases lined up on the gunbelt. He wished he had a gun like that.

'Jacob, you understand the difference between the truth and a lie, don't you, son?' the sheriff began.

'Yes, sir.'

'I'm going to ask you a few questions and I don't want no lies, you understand?'

'Yes, sir.'

'Were you in the house last night when the visitors called in?'

'Yes, sir.'

'Did you hear any arguing, raised voices or anything like that?'

Jacob's hands were beginning to sweat. He had barely had any contact with the sheriff in his ten years of life. Once, the sheriff had come out to the ranch when there had been rustlers, about a year ago, but he couldn't remember any other times. He linked his hands in front of him, rubbing the palms together, then dropped his arms to his sides.

'Yes, sir.'

'Do you know what the argument was about?'

'About the ranch I think, and my mum, and . . .' he trailed off, trying to remember the words, but all he could hear were the screams and the punches. He put his hands to his ears to shut out the noise, but all it did was to keep it in.

Sheriff Hart reached across and moved Jacob's hands away from his ears. He continued with the questions, not aggressive but persistent.

'Where were you when this was going on?'

'In our bedroom.'

'And did you hear any shooting?'

'Yes, sir.'

'Who fired the gun?'

Jacob shook his head.

'How many shots did you hear?'

'Two.' He was very clear about that, or was he? 'I think there were two shots and a lot of noise.'

'And you stayed in the bedroom all the time?'

'No, sir, I had to get my sister out or they would have found us.'

'Where did you go?'

Jacob knew he wasn't to tell anyone about the hiding place, his pa had told him that if he did it wouldn't be any use any more. Jacob decided he couldn't even tell the sheriff.

'Outside.'

'Outside?' queried the sheriff. 'Tell me where, sonny?'

'We hid in the shed.'

'So you didn't hear anything else?'

'No, sir.'

The sheriff looked him in the eye and decided there was nothing more to be gleaned. 'Cut along, then, Jacob.'

The boy turned to go but hesitated by the door. 'Can I see my pa?'

'I guess so. Come along later to my office.'

'Thank you, sir.'

Jacob left the room and closed the door but he could hear John talking, so he paused and pressed his ear to the gap in the doorframe. '. . . witness,' John was saying.

'Nothing at all,' replied the sheriff. 'There ain't the slightest chance anyone would make anything of that. No, it looks pretty clear-cut to me. When we got out there Zachary was almost passed out with the liquor. The gun was still in his hand. I guess he'd lost his temper, fired a couple of shots at Ambrose and killed Tod instead. I think he must have given Rebecca a beating after Ambrose and Clem left. The doc says she might not pull through, so she ain't goin' to be no use as a witness. The boy just said the arguing was about the ranch and his mum. Everyone knows Ambrose was keen on Rebecca before she married Zach. Ambrose admitted he told Zach he was seeing Rebecca.'

'I don't believe that,' Abigail said. It was the first time she had spoken. 'Rebecca goin' behind Zachary's back? No, she wouldn't never have done that. She loved her husband and she loved her kids. No sir, that ain't right—'

The sheriff cut in. 'Ambrose swears she came to see him, secretly, and more than once and she was pleading with him, offered him anything he wanted. Now I know Ambrose Sandford ain't a popular man round here; too much money and too much power, but his side of the story hangs together pretty good.'

Abigail fell silent; she couldn't believe what she was hearing. The sheriff sucked in some air.

'Seems like reason enough for Zachary to give her a beating, an' being drunk he didn't know when to stop. Well, I'd best be getting back. You can bring the boy along to see his pa later this afternoon. I need to get some more answers out of Zach when he's completely sober. Must say I didn't know Zach was a heavy drinker. But you can never tell how folk react to bad news, or a cheatin' wife. Anyways the judge'll be here in Beckinson in a couple of weeks. It's for him to decide if Zach should stand trial.'

Jacob heard the sheriff getting up out of his chair, so he skedaddled through the kitchen and out of the back door into the yard. Rachel was sitting on an upturned box, talking to a rag doll that Abigail had found for her.

'This is Emily,' Rachel said. 'Emily, this is my brother, Jacob. We'll ask him when we're going home. Jacob, when are we going home?'

'I dunno, Rachey. The sheriff says I can go and see Pa this afternoon.'

'Can I come? Emily wants to meet our pa.'

But Jacob didn't answer; he was churning some sentences in his head. It sounded like the sheriff thought his pa was the one who'd given his ma a beating. But it wasn't like that. Rachel spoke directly to the doll.

'You see, Emily, boys are so rude they don't even answer your questions when you speak to them.'

Jacob was pacing in the yard, looking down at his feet. His head was already too full of questions to take in any more.

Sheriff Hart's head was also filled with a jumble of questions. He took a chair through to the cells and placed it outside the one where Zachary Peterson was lying on a straw mattress and facing the wall. He put the chair down on the stone floor with a loud clatter, hoping Zachary would stir. He did. He groaned and turned over.

'Zach, I need to ask you a few questions. Are you listenin'? How are you feelin' right now?'

Zachary eased himself up on an elbow.

'I don't rightly know, Hal. My head's spinning.'

'You hit the bottle a bit hard last night. Couldn't get any sense out of you at all.'

Zach looked at the sheriff with bleary eyes.

'What am I doin' in here? Hal Hart? What's goin' on? I ain't never been in your cells before.'

'Perhaps you never shot a man before. Or beat up a woman.'

'What?' Zachary's eyes narrowed and his brow furrowed with disbelief. 'Beat up a woman? Me?'

'Not just any woman, Zach. Your wife, Rebecca.'

'What?'

'Within an inch of her life. The doc's patched her up but it's an even chance she isn't goin' to pull through. And as for Tod, he's stone-cold dead.'

'Tod?'

'Tod Martin, Clem's brother. Ambrose Sandford's men. You shot him.'

'*I* shot him?'

'Twice, once in the leg and another in the chest to finish him off. You still had the gun in your hand when we found you. You must have gone loco, there was blood everywhere. I imagine you were sore about Rebecca goin' with Ambrose an' all. Was that why you beat her?'

'Rebecca goin' with Ambrose?'

'Well I guess a jury might overlook that – unless she don't recover, of course. But Judge Chainey's goin' to have to decide about you killin' Tod. You might claim self-defence,

19

an' a jury of townsfolk will surely let you off; you're a good man Zach and you ain't done nothin' like this before. Anyways, sleep it off an' we'll talk some more.'

Zachary couldn't grasp what was going on. The skinful of whiskey had dulled his senses, his memory, his whole life, really. His head was throbbing and he struggled to make any sense of the conversation he had just had.

Ambrose Sandford sat down in the studded leather armchair. Clem Martin poured a glass of whiskey and handed it to him. Sandford took a cigar out of the box and lit it. Between puffs, as the end started to glow, he spoke through his teeth, rolling the cigar round his mouth.

'Well, you wanted Tod out of the way, and it's done. The claim will have to be made over to you as sole owner, and the mine will be yours. I'll get a lawyer on to it right away. You won't have to share the inheritance with your brother an' Zachary Peterson'll hang for the murder. Couldn't be better. You get the silver mine in your own name and I'll get the Peterson ranch. That'll give us the access road to the mine across the Peterson land. A neat plan, neatly done.'

Clem Martin took a slug of his whiskey.

'And you get the woman.'

Sandford nodded. 'Yep, I get the woman.'

Martin continued. 'Only if a jury convicts Peterson. It looks like the sheriff bought our story, lock, stock an' barrel, but Zachary Peterson hasn't got any enemies. He'll claim self-defence when he realizes what's happened, and there ain't no jury going to hang a man for self-defence.'

Sandford thought for a moment.

'When are you goin' to see your ma and tell her what's happened?'

'It'll take four or five days for a round trip. And she won't take it too good, Tod was always her favourite.'

'Does she keep money in the house?'

'Pa always used to, quite a lot in the safe.'

'Can you bring back twelve hundred dollars?

'Twelve hundred!' Clem exclaimed.

'For twelve good men and true, who know what verdict to return.'

'But you shot him; why don't you pay for a jury? You're the one gettin' off the rope.'

Sandford shook his head. 'I don't benefit none from your silver mine. Not yet, anyway. With Tod out of the way that's your good fortune, Clem. I simply done what you didn't want to do yourself. That's what we agreed.' He blew a long stream of thick white cigar smoke into the room.

Clem finished off the whiskey. He didn't like the way Sandford had everything worked out, but he would bide his time.

'In that case I better saddle up and make a start.'

Clem Martin closed the door behind him. Ambrose Sandford sat back in his chair. He smiled to himself and with good reason. Things were working out pretty.

'Pretty good,' he said out loud, taking himself by surprise. 'Three, four, mebbe five years' time and this town and everything in it will belong to me.'

## 3

The cream of Chicago society would never go to a major civic event without a visit to Clifford and Leila Burlen's clothing store on West Market Street. It was the only place where the latest fashions from Paris could not only be seen in the catalogues but, more important, actually made up on the premises to the highest of standards. The regular shipments of fine materials from the old world often sold out as soon as they arrived. This was just as well, as there is nothing so transitory as fashion.

A major civic reception had recently been held and Clifford Burlen was looking through the stockroom to see what was left from the new French fabrics. By his side was his twenty-year-old nephew, Jacob Peterson, whose name had been changed to Jacob Burlen. He was carefully writing down the figures as Clifford called them out.

'Fine cotton cambric, purple and white stripes, item 25/246, two bolts; a glazed cotton cambric, simple crimson stripe, item 25/247, ten bolts. You know, Jacob, I'm surprised we've got that much left of that one. Let's hope it stays in fashion a while longer.'

'You could always ship it out West, Uncle,' Jacob suggested. 'We're always being asked by agents.'

Clifford was a shrewd businessman in his late forties, thin and pale from a lifetime spent indoors with frequent running up and down the stairs in his substantial four-storey brick-built premises. He'd built up the business with his wife. Leila, who shared selling space on the ground floor for her millinery. On the first floor they employed a small army of local girls to make up the hats, dresses, bodices, corsets and every kind of garment you could think of. On the third floor was kept the stock of fabrics and other construction materials, such as the miles of thread on wooden cones in a range of thicknesses and colours. There were bone and wooden stiffeners, feathers, trimmings, buttons, hooks, catches and fastenings of every description. Bolts of fabric, no longer in fashion, were consigned to the dusty fourth floor at the top.

Jacob's sister, Rachel, had been learning the millinery side of the business under Leila's expert guidance as soon as she could handle a needle and thread. Now, at the age of fifteen, she was one of the most creative designers in Leila's workshop and practically in charge of the innovations department. At such a young age that might have caused resentment, but her happy disposition and considerate manners ensured that there was no enmity towards her amongst the older employees.

Jacob too had been absorbing every aspect of the business, shadowing Clifford from almost the very first day of being welcomed into the Burlen's household.

With no children of their own, Leila and Clifford had doted on their two young relatives, helping them to come to terms with their bouts of tearfulness and disturbing nightmares. Gradually, over the years, they had become like any other happy family, working hard and reaping the rewards of a successful business in a time of booming trade. A smart young man with a keen intellect and intelligent, enquiring deep-brown eyes that missed no details, Jacob knew pretty much everything about merchandising fine fabrics, wholesale and retail. It was unusual, though, for him to share his opinions with his uncle.

'Sell them to agents out West, Uncle. Clear the old stock.'

Yes, I heard what you said, I was thinking about it. I could,' agreed Clifford, 'but who would I trust to handle the company's business?'

'A manager?'

'There isn't anyone I know who could do it.'

'I would,' said Jacob, on the spur of the moment without thinking about what he was saying. 'Rachel and me. We could do it. Together we could. I was just ten years old, Uncle, when you took us in after Ma and Pa . . . after that long trek across country by stage and train, and all the strangeness of life in the East. You and Aunt Leila couldn't have been kinder to us.'

'Your ma was Leila's sister.'

'Yes I know and I thank God for it, and I thank God for your kindness to us, so does Rachel. Well, I'm twenty now and I've learned the business well. . . .'

'That's certainly true.'

'And Rachel makes swell hats.'

'She certainly does.'

'And it makes good business sense, expanding out West. We're always hearing about the lack of the latest fashions in the cattle towns and the mining towns. There's plenty of money out there and nothing to spend it on. That's why some of our customers are buying quarter-bolts and sending them to family out there. Leastways, that's what they say.'

'Yes, I know there's trade to be had.' Clifford was ruminating. 'But the West is so backward, uncivilized; why would you want to go back that way when the future is here in the East? This is where you'll make your fortune – and you know this business will be yours one day.'

'Yes, I know, Uncle.' But the spirit of adventure was rising in him. 'Could you give me, say, five years to try and establish a business in one of the growing towns out West? I'll double your investment.'

'Ever the optimist! But if anyone could do it I reckon you could. I'll give it some thought and see what your aunt thinks. Now let's press on. Here's a fine linen lawn, 25/248, plain white for starching, about thirty yards only. Come on, Jacob, write that down. There's work to be done here.'

Jacob wrote down the figures automatically; his mind was not on the rolls of cloth – an entirely different plan was formulating itself in his mind. It was building on something which had been dormant for years but was beginning to smoulder in his head, like a volcano heating up. The prospect of running his own business with his uncle's backing was very exciting. The more he thought about it, the more it appealed. He was sure Rachel would be keen. Seeing the way she moulded and teased the blank felt into fine shapes, then covered them with silks and ribbons, he was sure she would be a success wherever they went.

He was confident he could talk his aunt and uncle into backing the scheme. All he would have to do would be to choose a suitable town in which to set up shop. Already he knew where that would be.

The next three months went by in a tornado of activity. Once his uncle and aunt had agreed to the scheme Jacob set about the detail of his plans. Rachel was over the moon with excitement, if a little tearful at times at the thought of leaving their comfortable and happy existence. Such a speculative journey, but she knew that once her brother had set his mind on something there was no going back.

'But where are we going to live?' was Rachel's most pressing question. Jacob sought to calm her.

'Uncle Clifford has arranged a hotel until we can find a house to rent. He sent a wire to a land agent and he's been assured that there are suitable premises empty or newly under construction that will suit our business.'

'And how long is it going to take us to travel across country?'

'Only a matter of days; not like before.'

This time they would cover the distance mostly by rail, first to the bustling town of Cheyenne, then changing for the southern route to Denver. From there they would have to suffer the uncomfortable travel by stage to their new home in Beckinson. Ten years ago the war was not long ended and the journey away from Beckinson for the two children by stage-coach had been tiring and emotional. Rachel had cried most of the way, although she hardly knew why, and everywhere they stayed seemed full of soldiers, horses, baggage trains and every kind of traffic that got in the way, making their journey twice as long. Then, arriving in Chicago had seemed like entering another world with its massive buildings, wide streets, vibrant population, dust, dirt and noise.

After the terrifying fire of '71 Chicago had begun to rise again in stone, brick and steel. *Burlen's Haberdashery* moved to its present four-storey premises on West Market Street, next to the newly created municipal park, and the family, Clifford and Leila, with their two adopted child relatives, Jacob and Rachel, moved into a fine new villa out of the city centre. Now Jacob was about to give up all that for an uncertain future in the foothills of the Rocky Mountains. Rachel had no recollection of snow-covered mountains; indeed, they could only be seen in the distance from Beckinson, but she fervently hoped they wouldn't be as bitingly windy as the winter streets of Chicago.

Clifford and Jacob spent many days discussing the minutiae of business matters such as financial arrangements, stock control and the vexing question of regular supplies. About a week before the due date of departure they were sitting together one night in the front parlour after a sumptuous turkey dinner with pies and jellies and French wines, when Clifford said he had something to give to Jacob. He left the room and returned with a small tin trunk the size of a large hatbox.

'Do you remember this box?'

Jacob looked at it carefully.

'Can't say that I do. Wait a minute . . . isn't that. . . .'

'Yes, the one you brought in your luggage.'

'I've no idea what's in it.' Jacob said with a laugh, but then his expression changed to one of melancholy. 'Oh! Isn't it the one that belonged to Pa?'

Clifford unlocked the box and opened it for Jacob to see the contents.

'It was all that he left: the possessions which your pa, my brother-in-law Zachary, wanted you to have. There's a note somewhere.'

Jacob lifted the envelope out of the box; it was addressed to him personally, Jacob Peterson. Having taken the surname Burlen when they were formally adopted by their aunt and uncle, seeing the old name and remembering who he once was pricked tears in Jacob's eyes.

Inside the envelope was a short note which had been written by Beckinson's Pastor Creeley, as his pa couldn't write. Inside the box were three items: a silver pocket watch inscribed on the reverse, being a wedding present from Rebecca to Zachary; a finely tooled leather gunbelt and holster, being the largest item taking up most of the space, and underneath was an out-dated handgun. Jacob put the gunbelt aside and lifted the revolver from the box. The chambers were empty, of course. He held it loosely in his hand and his mind flashed back to the knothole in the wall, the rain lashing the window, the shouting and the shot – not one but two – and his pupils dilated at the remembrance of the second deafening noise so close to the bedroom door that the vibration shook the floorboards.

'I remember Pa had a rifle, a Spencer, but I suppose someone stole that.'

Clifford sighed. 'This was all that came from the sheriff's office in your luggage. This and another small box with some jewellery from you mother which Rachel must have. Should I give it to her before you go, or will you take it and give it to her when she's a little older?'

'Rachel *is* a little older; fifteen years doesn't seem that much, but she is almost a grown woman and she should have Ma's jewellery to wear whenever she wants . . .' Jacob paused in mid thought. 'Uncle, wasn't there Pa's wedding ring anywhere?'

'I guess not; it was probably buried with him.'

'Maybe. He never took it off, except once to show me the inside, where it said 'Zachary and Rebecca 1855'. Were you there, Clifford, when they got married?'

'Me, yes, I was just a friend of Leila at the time and we were both at her sister Rebecca's wedding.'

'Were they happy, Ma and Pa?' Jacob knew Clifford couldn't really answer that question since Zachary and Rebecca had moved out West quite soon after marrying, but he had to lay the ghostly rumour of his father beating his mother. He couldn't believe it had ever happened; it went against everything he knew, everything he'd seen in their happy home life on the ranch.

'I guess so,' Clifford said, having some idea of why Jacob had asked. 'They were devoted to each other. Now listen, tomorrow we'll go to the gunsmith and get you a decent piece to put in that holster. You can't go out West unarmed.'

'Those that live by the gun die by the gun,' Jacob remarked wisely. 'I'm not sure it's a good idea. I learned to use that Spencer on the ranch. Pa would line up some cans, put bullets in the tube, push it into the stock and hand me the gun. I'd shoot until the tube was empty, sometimes I'd actually hit a can. But I haven't fired anything since we came to Chicago.'

Nevertheless, the next day Jacob accompanied Clifford to Flint's gunsmith's, a few blocks away, and spent an hour handling different pieces to feel the weight and balance.

He was all for taking a small pocket pistol rather than something big enough to go in the holster but Clifford was insistent, so, after trying some in the shooting gallery at the back of the store, Jacob settled on a single-action Smith & Wesson .44, which was heavy but sturdy and reliable. It was expensive at twenty dollars.

'The Schofield. A fine choice,' Flint pronounced. 'It's Smith & Wesson's latest model, modified by Major Schofield and issued to the US army. You won't do better than that.'

That evening Jacob showed the gun to Rachel before packing it away with the gunbelt and holster. He had no intention of wearing it on the train, or indeed at any other time for that matter. He told her about the things in the box and the note from Pastor Creeley.

'You must use the watch,' Rachel said as she turned it over in her hand. She opened the little box of jewellery that Clifford had given her and took out a gold chain with a neatly worked solid-gold cross. The inscription on the back of the cross identified it as a wedding gift from Zachary to Rebecca.

'Just as I intend to wear this,' she added. She flicked up her long, chestnut hair and fastened the catch at the nape of her neck.

Three days later they were at the station, taking their leave of their aunt and uncle. In one of the baggage cars was the stack of packing-cases holding the starter stock which Clifford and Jacob had put together, along with several boxes of hat-making materials for Rachel. A trunk held most of their clothes and they each had a large carpetbag packed with essentials and a change of clothes for the overnight stops. It was a tearful parting, but once the train had pulled out of the station excitement began to replace apprehension.

Ten years after their tragic departure from Beckinson as

the orphaned Jacob and Rachel Peterson they were about to make the return journey as Jacob and Rachel Burlen, aspiring haberdashers.

Clifford had bought expensive tickets which ensured that they travelled in as much comfort as possible. The carriage was lined in figured mahogany. The spacious button-back seats were covered in red plush. Refreshments were served throughout the day, and the carriage was fitted with gaslights for night travel. How different from that horrendous journey by stagecoach which was now little more than a vague nightmarish recollection.

Even so, the standard-class carriages were packed with a noisy variety of folk travelling westwards, the majority of them heading for the silver strikes in the Black Hills, hoping to make their fortune.

Jacob and Rachel's final stop on that line was at Cheyenne, where they were booked into one of the city's hotels. Jacob supervised the unloading and overnight storage of their extensive baggage. Replete after a fine meal in the hotel's grand dining room they passed a pleasant evening in the ballroom, where a musical recital was being held. An early night beckoned as their train south to Denver was scheduled to depart early in the morning.

After breakfasting early on coffee, freshly baked bread, fruit and cheese Jacob hurried down to the station to make sure all their packing-cases were properly loaded. Clifford had warned him to be present every time the cases were loaded and unloaded to be sure of not losing anything. They had been boldly marked BURLEN and were numbered, so checking was quick and easy. Rachel arrived by carriage in good time for the departure. She held a handkerchief to her nose to ward off the overwhelming stench of cattle, which were noisy, smelly and constantly on the move around the vast marshalling yards. The air was full of dust and the loud lowing of disgruntled beeves. It was a relief to get on the train and watch Cheyenne disappear from view.

The journey to Denver passed through a variety of undulating pasture and mixed woodland. Progress was steady and the gentle rolling of the carriage almost lulled them to sleep.

'Look Jacob,' Rachel said, pointing out of the window. 'Riders. Three of them coming towards the train. No, look, more of them. There's four – five – six.'

Jacob turned to look at the riders and was immediately filled with a foreboding. They were galloping at the same speed as the train and pistols were drawn. The train was slowing. Passengers in the car began to look anxiously out of the window. A man at the front got up and tried to see if he could secure the door but there was no way of locking it. He turned to the worried faces.

'No guns, folks, just stay calm. They haven't come to murder us, but don't try to hide anything.'

'It's a raid,' Jacob said to Rachel. 'Sit quite still and don't do anything silly.' He was glad he wasn't wearing a gunbelt. A moment later the brakes were fully applied and the screeching of metal drowned out the shooting of guns and the shouting.

Rachel quickly unfastened the catch on her gold neck-chain.

'Give me your pocket watch. *Quick*, Jacob.'

Jacob took it out of his coat pocket and handed it over. Rachel snatched it away and discreetly slipped her hand under her skirt and into her drawers.

The carriage door burst open and a burly man strode into the carriage waving a gun. A loose bandanna was pulled up over the lower half of his face. He fired a shot into the roof.

'Hold 'em high! Just sit still and nobody gets hurt.'

**4**

The masked bandit waved the revolver, making sure that everyone's hands went compliantly up in the air.

'Now ladies, have your jewellery ready – and be quick.'He fired another shot into the roof; it made an ear-splitting blast. The acrid smell of black powder filled the carriage and people started to cough and sneeze. The robber searched coat-pockets and bags, working his way down the carriage. Folk said nothing, knowing a wrong or disrespectful word might end in sudden death. A second man came into the car with a bag to take the loot. Most of his face was also covered, but Jacob was struck by his very pale-blue, piercing eyes, which darted all round the carriage.

Suddenly there was a commotion; a man was forced to get up and take his shoes off – the robber suspected that he had hidden his wife's jewellery. The shoe was snatched away.

'Goddam sonofabitch!' the bandit bawled, emptying some rings and a gold chain into his hand. Then he aimed his gun at one of the man's stockinged feet and fired a shot. The man hollered with pain, fainted and fell to the floor. Women screamed and put their hands to their ears to ease the reverberating sound of yet another gunshot. It was a dreadful warning to everyone. It seemed the robbers were only after cash and jewellery. Then Jacob suddenly thought of their valuable cargo in the baggage car. It would be the

32

end of their venture if they were to lose all that.

When the two men got to Jacob one searched his coat pockets and found nothing. His gaunt, stubbly face came close to Jacob's and his breath smelt of liquor.

'No money, no watch, no nuthin'? No bags?'

Jacob stood up and pointed to the two carpetbags on the luggage rack.

'And what about you, miss? No jewellery? Are you two paupers? How d'yer buy tickets to travel in this comfort?'

'Our uncle paid for the tickets,' Jacob said plainly.

The man looked him up and down, then made Jacob take his shoes off. He found nothing.

'They're only youngsters,' said the other man, but the first man wasn't finished. He turned to Rachel who was still sitting calmly.

'Get your bag down, miss.'

She pointed to it and it was lifted down. Rachel opened it up and took out a clean pair of drawers.

'Perhaps you'd like these?' she said sarcastically.

The man snatched the garment from her and lewdly pressed his hand on her posterior.

'To remind me of you!' he said vilely.

'Don't be so disgusting—' Jacob began. The man rounded on him and hit him across the face.

Just then the car door opened and another robber, his bandanna pulled up over his face, called his accomplices off in a grating, high-pitched voice. They left.

The tension eased. The passengers looked out of the window. A couple of shots were fired from further down the train but the bandits were well out of range. Some of the women started sobbing at the loss of their jewellery, while their husbands were doing their best to provide some comfort. The injured man was being bandaged but he looked very pale. Rachel was dabbing at Jacob's jaw, which was bleeding; although he found it excruciatingly painful as she touched it, luckily nothing seemed to be broken.

'Welcome to the West,' he managed to mouth to Rachel despite the pain. He put his arms round her to comfort her. 'I'm sorry I've brought you to this.'

'I'm fine and dandy,' she replied. 'You're the one who took a risk. I thought he was about to shoot you.' She turned her back briefly, fumbled under her skirt, then handed him his watch.

'That was a smart move,' Jacob admitted. 'I wouldn't have thought of that.'

'Not even a vile bandit would dare to search there,' she said.

The conductor came into the car to check on the passengers. He took a look at the wounded man who was lying along the length of a seat, covered with a blanket and being comforted by his distraught wife. The conductor promised medical help at Denver.

The train began to build up a head of steam and at last pulled away. The rest of the journey was completed in an air of quiet relief, everybody glad that nobody had been killed. One passenger said that only a couple of weeks ago three people had been shot in a raid and two of them had died, yet the train company still weren't putting armed men on every train and something ought to be done about it.

Denver was a welcome sight. It was an impressive town built of brick and stone, its wide streets bustling with commercial activity. The coming of the railway had encouraged speculation, so new buildings were springing up all round. Judging by the number of travellers on the train it was also becoming a popular stopping place for tourists who wanted to visit the wonders of the Rocky Mountains. That probably accounted for the easy pickings on the train: tourists travel with cash and jewellery. The train company would have to do something to make the railroad safer, but rumours of rich veins of silver were bringing prospectors in their droves. The railway provided a link with the rest of the Union, making the mountains more accessible; some of them were nearly as high as the hopes of the miners.

All this was good news for Jacob. He was convinced that people would have money to spend in high-class stores. When he and Rachel left the train to put up at the hotel he rather wished they were setting up shop in this bustling metropolis. Maybe one day, but right now there was a higher priority on his mind.

Jacob spent the following day with a freight merchant at Quincey's warehouse arranging for the carriage of their stock to Beckinson, which was just about thirty miles into the western foothills. The passenger stagecoach to Beckinson wasn't due to leave for a couple of days, so he and Rachel enjoyed the delights of Denver and visited every haberdasher, milliner and clothing store to see what was being offered and what people were buying. Prices were higher than Jacob had expected and the fashions were at least a season behind what Clifford was offering in Chicago. Prospects looked good; Jacob was convinced that their enterprise would be successful.

Three days later they checked into one of Beckinson's two hotels on Main Street, The Silver Dollar. The town had grown considerably. Jacob found it almost unrecognizable. Gone were the pine-clad false façades, the rickety board-walks and Sheriff Hart's old office. They had all been replaced with neat brick buildings, substantial wooden premises and decent wooden boardwalks raised well above the dusty street.

New hardware stores, a bank, two mining-claims agents, a real-estate broker, several attorneys, dining rooms, a laundry, two groceries, two saloons, a barber's shop and a newspaper office clustered at the town centre. But Jacob's eye alighted on a fine, empty, double-fronted shop slap bang opposite the bank. It had two glass display windows, exactly the right kind for showing dressed mannequins. Close by, the sheriff's grand new office was twice the size of the old one, making its presence felt on the street.

Main Street itself was now twice as long and full of commercial properties as far as the eye could see. The town was alive with comings and goings. Silver mines in the surrounding hills had evidently increased its prosperity.

Beckinson even had its share of Rocky Mountain tourism, served not just by the two hotels but also a tour office, advertising day trips into the mountains, with deer-hunting and waterfall-sightseeing.

As they settled into their hotel suite at The Silver Dollar Jacob gave Rachel a hug. 'This is the right place for us to grow our business.'

'I still don't understand why we've come to Beckinson instead of setting up in Denver. That looked a mighty fine place to me. We could do well there. I don't know why, but this place makes me feel sad.'

Jacob glossed over this last remark. 'We could never have brought enough stock with us to start up in a big city like Denver. Uncle Clifford couldn't risk that much in a new venture. If we build a business here, then in a year or two – or maybe three at most, I promise we'll move to Denver.'

Jacob knew that Denver would be the best place, but they had had to come to Beckinson first. There was business to be done in Beckinson. A new business to be started and old business to be finished.

It took just two weeks for Jacob to conclude a deal on the empty shop. The property had been vacated only the previous month and there had been interest from other businesses, but the land agent, Dexter Gray, had immediately taken a liking to Jacob.

'Well, Mr Burlen—' Dexter Gray began.

'I'd prefer Jacob.'

'Indeed, Jacob,' Gray acknowledged, pushing the papers across the desk. 'I need your signature down here, and here, and here.'

Jacob dipped the pen into the ink and neatly signed his name.

Along with all the other things that Clifford and Leila had given him, three years of good education had enabled Jacob to master all the social accomplishments he was ever likely to need, and although Rachel hadn't been given the same formal schooling Leila had taught her to read and write at home. They were both well qualified to become pillars of society.

'That's all done, now here are the keys for you,' Gray continued. 'The people of Beckinson will be very pleased to see a haberdasher taking over the store, not least, of course, all the wives who will be flocking to spend their husbands' dollars.' He laughed. 'Mine included!'

'That's exactly why we've chosen Beckinson.'

'Well perhaps my wife . . . we came here about six years ago, just when one or two local mining claims were beginning to produce good results. I thought there'd be good business in property. I bought up a few plots and I'm glad I did. Now, a word of advice: it's worth being on good terms with the important people in town, people like Mr Martin and Mr Sandford who own the bank. Anyway, you'll probably meet them soon enough.'

'When we're ready for business send your wife along, Mr Gray. We'll take her as the first customer and fit her out with a dress of the finest silk in a colour and style of her own choosing. She'll be the talk of the town. It will be our gift for our successful negotiation on the lease.'

Jacob went back to the hotel for Rachel and together they strolled down to their new premises. After turning the key he let Rachel open the door and be the first one in.

'This wall will be shelved to hold the bolts of fabric,' he said. Rachel was not to be outdone.

'The window on my side will show a collection of hats, and we'll have two chairs here for customers to sit and admire themselves in the mirrors fixed to the wall.'

'And on my side of the shop,' Jacob went on, 'I'll need a glass-topped display counter so customers can see the range of items—'

Rachel didn't let him finish his sentence. 'You and I will be master and mistress upstairs,' she said, crossing to the broad stairway which went up to the living quarters on the first floor. There was still a great deal to do before the place would be ready for them to move in and open their doors to the Beckinson clientele, but they couldn't help being gripped by a sudden excitement as they sized up the premises.

It was high summer and the sun was beating down on to the baked dust of Main Street. A big old cottonwood provided some shade near the sheriff's office. The time of year for the move had been carefully planned so that trading would be well under way for the fall season and ladies would be ordering their winter wardrobe for the dances and functions that occupied the long winter nights.

Having breakfasted in the hotel Jacob left Rachel measuring up with local carpenters in the shop and strolled across to the bank to set up the details of the trading account and the transfer of funds from Chicago. His appointment was at ten o'clock with the manager, Randall Tarne.

There hadn't been a bank in Beckinson when they'd lived there before. As far as Jacob could remember his pa had usually kept money at the ranch or deposited larger sums with an attorney when he had to settle bills. Some people had used the general store as a kind of bank, especially for credit. Now, fronted by two imposing pillars and a stone portico, there was a fine brick-built bank with iron bars across the windows,. It was a mark of the town's new prosperity.

A finely painted sign proclaimed:

## SANDFORD'S BANK
Open for Deposits, loans at low rates and insurances
of all kinds

Above the door, chiselled into the lintel stone, were the names of the proprietors: Ambrose Sandford and Clem Martin, and the founding date, May 23 1866.

The heavy polished oak door was open. Jacob walked up to the enquiry counter.

'Good morning, my name's Burlen, Jacob Burlen. I have an appointment with the manager.'

A door behind the counter opened and a man came across to the desk.

'Mr Burlen? Good morning, sir. I thought I heard your name. Spot on ten o'clock, very punctual.' He held a hand out vaguely in Jacob's direction. 'Randall Tarne, manager. Would you like to come through?'

The opulence of the manager's office indicated that the bank was securely funded. Either that, or its customers were being charged extortionately high rates of interest.

Manager Randall Tarne was a thin man in his late forties, perhaps early fifties. His hair was greying at the temples. Behind thick glasses his eyes were soft and kindly, yet distant. He waited for Jacob to speak.

'Has the bank been established long?' Jacob asked, despite having seen the 1866 foundation inscription above the door.

'Ten years. We had a celebration earlier this year, with a

big reception, a banquet and dance for the residents of the town. It's a shame you weren't here then, Mr Burlen. The ladies were eager to spend money on new fabrics and dresses, but there was very little choice.'

'And I presume the reserves are secure?'

'Oh yes, it's fully backed by a silver mine.'

'The bank owns a mine?' Jacob wondered.

'Mr Martin owns the mine: he's one of the proprietors. He's often in town. He is always interested in the new businesses that want to set up here. I understand your sister makes hats?'

'Yes, a significant part of the business will be hers. So, Mr Martin owns a silver mine. What about Mr Sandford? Does he own a mine too?'

'No sir, Mr Sandford is more interested in real estate. He's the mayor, as you probably know; he owns the two hotels, the two saloons and has many other interests in the town.'

*I bet he does,* Jacob thought.

'He used to raise beef,' Tarne continued, 'but with the mining boom he moved into a more lucrative line of business. I understand there had been some land deals a long time ago; he bought up a lot of the other local beef concerns and then sold out to a meat-packing company in Denver. Now they're planning to open a branch of the bank in Denver itself.'

Jacob had heard as much as he needed to know for the moment. He moved the conversation on to his own banking arrangements, agreed the details, then got up.

'Well, thank you, Mr Tarne, that's been most interesting. What about yourself? Have you lived here long?'

'Me? Oh no, I'm still an outsider; we've only been here a couple of years, my wife Amelia and myself. I moved from Denver to be the manager of this bank, sought out and appointed by Mr Sandford himself – he made me the deputy mayor, in fact.'

'Perhaps you'll be going back to Denver to manage the new bank?' Jacob hazarded.

Randall Tarne simply smiled modestly, shrugged his shoulders and raised his eyebrows. 'Maybe.'

'Well, I look forward to welcoming your wife into our shop.'

They shook hands. It was a more agreeable meeting than Jacob had expected. Randall Tarne was a newcomer; there was no reason to suspect him of any involvement in the past despite his association with Sandford and Martin. Tarne was simply a banker, it seemed. Sandford and Martin would have seen the merit in bringing in people who knew nothing of how they had operated in the past.

Jacob needed to find out more about Martin's silver mine, but he had a fair idea about what had happened to his parents' ranch with its prime grazing. It was now part of some larger Denver business. There was a lot to find out.

A visit to Sheriff Hart was next on Jacob's list.

# 5

On entering the sheriff's office he was struck by the number of lawmen lounging around. Sheriff Hart had managed the town all by himself, now he could see three or four men wearing badges.

'I'm looking for Sheriff Hart,' Jacob said confidently.

'Well you're in the wrong place,' came the reply from behind a big oak desk. The man got up and introduced himself. 'I'm the sheriff here, Curtis O'Donnel, Hal Hart left some years back. Shot in the bank raid. Retired soon after.'

'Bank raid?' Jacob queried.

O'Donnel nodded. 'Yes, about three or four years ago.'

'More like six,' corrected one of the deputies.

'Maybe,' agreed the sheriff. 'There was a raid and a gun battle, Hart was badly injured. He survived but moved away afterwards.' He turned to one of the deputies. 'Where was it he went? Down to Denver, wasn't it?'

'Somewhere near there,' replied the deputy. 'A little place called Crossing Point, I believe.'

When Jacob met up with his sister for lunch he desperately wanted to tell her the things he had found out, but he knew he couldn't. He felt slightly treacherous, since they had always shared all their thoughts and plans, but it would be unfair to burden her with things she couldn't possibly remember. Things which only he could deal with. There were only two names on the list in his mind, Sandford and Martin. He was sure Hal Hart would know the others.

They ate their lunch in a restaurant on Main Street, making mental notes of exactly what everyone was wearing. It was a habit of business, and they shared quiet comment on the state of sartorial elegance in Beckinson. There was definite room for improvement; many of the men's suits looked a little tired and the ladies' attire was distinctly two or three seasons old.

'I'm going to be away a couple of days, Rachel.'

'No matter,' she said cheerily, 'there's plenty for me to do keeping the shop fittings on schedule. I've heard about some display cabinets going for sale at a store that's moving to Denver. I'll go and have a look at them this afternoon.'

'I've arranged a horse at the livery and I'll be making a start after lunch. You'll be all right on your own?'

'Sure,' she said. 'You take care too.'

Jacob had expected questions about where he was going but Rachel was too absorbed in thinking about the business.

The sun was still warm and a light breeze was blowing dust along Main Street as Jacob steered his hired mount round the conglomeration of carts and buggies. It was good to see the town so busy. Jacob was sure their venture would be a success. He rode on, deep in thought with ideas about the business, and it was mid evening when he arrived at the small farming community of Crossing Point down on the plain. The little settlement took its name from the meeting place of the river and the main route into Denver, which crossed on a sturdy wooden bridge. The one and only hostelry advertised rooms at cheap rates and fine home cooking. Jacob stabled the horse and, having taken a room for the night, sat down to a hearty dinner of beef pie with potatoes and vegetables. Tomorrow he would find Hal Hart.

\*

After a good breakfast of eggs and a thick slab of smoked pork, leisurely conversation with the proprietor had identified the Harts' place as a small ranch with a few horses and chickens, about a mile and a half downstream. By midmorning Jacob was mounted up and on his way. It was a matter of minutes before he came across the place. It seemed very peaceful. A woman was throwing corn on the ground, surrounded by a clucking entourage of pecking hens.

Jacob raised his hat.

'Mornin', ma'am.'

She looked up and shielded her eyes. She was older than he had expected with silver-grey hair done tightly in a bun. She stopped throwing corn and walked over to the gate.

'I'm looking for Hal Hart. I was told this was his place.'

She looked at him a long while, taking in every detail of his face.

'And what's your business with him, young feller?' It wasn't said in a belligerent manner, just curious.

'I wanted some information from him, about an incident a few years back when he was sheriff of Beckinson.'

'Beckinson!' she exclaimed. 'Why, I thought we'd finished with all that.'

'The bank raid? No, ma'am, this was long before, nothing to do with you moving away. I don't think so anyway.'

'Well, you'd better come in, I s'pose. The least I can do is make you some coffee. Have you eaten?'

Jacob slid off his horse hitched it to the fence and unlatched the gate.

'Leave your boots by the door, young man, and come inside.'

The furnishing was sparse; the curtains were quaint but

of plain homespun material, there was a checked cloth over the main table, the chairs were past their best and there was a lingering odour of vegetable stew. It didn't feel like a prosperous household.

'I guess Mr Hart's already out with the horses,' Jacob said lightly.

She was pouring boiling water from an enamel jug off the range into a coffee pot. She hesitated, then without looking at him said:

'My husband died two years ago, sonny. They got him eventually one way or another, the dirty skunks.'

'I'm sorry to hear that.'

She continued to fix the coffee. 'Hal was a good man. He upheld the law proper. Never did nothing wrong. Not until that trial . . . well, he never spoke about it but I knew it was eating him up. He told me he'd had no choice, there was nothing he could do in the face of such corruption.'

She brought a cup of coffee across to Jacob and put it on a table at his side.

'It wasn't to do with a hanging was it?' asked Jacob.

'How did you know that?'

'Was the bank raid and gunfight to do with that as well?'

'Yes – everything was to do with it. Beckinson was never the same after the trial. Hal kept it all quiet but eventually, after about four years had passed, he couldn't live with the lies so he rode into Denver when the judge was on his circuit. He told him straight the trial had been a farce, it was fixed, all the jurymen had been bought and paid for, and everyone of them had perjured himself to send that poor innocent man to the gallows. Peterson, Zachary Peterson. It was a wicked thing what they done, and Hal never got it out of his head.'

'You mean the man was innocent?'

'As innocent as the day is long. Zachary Peterson was no murderer, no more was he a wife-beater. It was all a put-up job and Hal could do nothin' 'bout it.'

'But he was the sheriff,' Jacob said, trying to understand how a lawman hadn't upheld the law.

'His hands were tied,' she said, with a sad look in her eye. 'He tried to make some amends. Are you sure I can trust you, young feller?'

'Yes, ma'am, on my word of honour.'

She broke off for a moment of reflection, rocking gently.

'Well, one night he was sitting in his office and there was a commotion out in the street. It looked like a raid on the bank. There was a group of masked men outside Sandford's Bank, bashing away at the door. Hal said it was just to get him out in the street, because they shot him as soon as he came out of the office, then rode away like cowardly skunks. That wasn't no bank raid.'

'But they didn't manage to kill him?' Jacob guessed.

She rocked herself to and fro in the big stickback rocker for a moment, her lips pursed. The floor creaked as the chair moved backwards and forwards, a clock ticked loudly on the shelf above the fireplace.

'Just winged him. Winged him bad in the shoulder and the leg. I nursed him back but he never had proper use again. He knew he had to get out of Beckinson or be killed, so we moved down here and raised a few horses. Then one day I found him on the ground out in the yard, stone-cold dead, kicked in the stomach by a horse. That's how it looked.'

'But. . . ?'

'But they done it somehow.'

'They?'

She got up out of the rocker and crossed the room to a writing desk.

'Hal gave me a list of names after he was shot and said it was some of these tried to kill him.' She rummaged through the desk and shuffled through scraps of paper. 'He said if they came back and killed him I was to give the list to an honest lawman. They all deserved to die. It's in a box in this drawer.'

'A list? Did you give it to anyone?'

'Dang! There ain't no list in the box, so I must have. Hal weren't kicked by no horse, that was cold-blooded murder. I thought I'd kept that piece of paper. Are you a lawman? You look too young for that.'

Jacob thought quickly.

'No, ma'am, I'm no lawman. I read about it in a newspaper and I thought I'd follow up the story.'

'It won't do no good raking it up after all these years. It's best left where it is. You're with a newspaper?' she asked.

'Kind of, with the *Clarion* in Beckinson,' Jacob said, blushing a bit for the lie. She peered closely at him, her eyes didn't focus too good.

'Matter of fact,' she said, 'you could try findin' the two young kids. They'd know about it. A boy an' a girl. Sweet little thing, Rachel was her name. Long curls that glistened in the sunshine, the colour of polished rose-gold. Don't remember the boy's name: Joseph, I think – or Jack, sumpin' like that. 'Course, when their ma was found in the river they were left homeless. Ma and pa gone in the space of seven days. Hal wanted us to look after them, but eventually they went off somewhere East. Philadelphia I think.'

Jacob pondered for a moment on the kind-heartedness of such folk: good honest folk, the salt of the earth on which civilized nations can be built.

'What was your name, sonny?'

'Jacob Burlen, ma'am.'

'Jacob! Yes, that was the boy's name, Jacob. Jacob Peterson. Fine-lookin' boy he was. Must be a grown man by now.'

Jacob got up before any more recollections came back to

the old lady.

'I want to thank you, ma'am; you've been a great help.'

'Would you like some more coffee? Plenty more in the pot. Nobody ever asked me about that hanging until you. Are you a trustworthy fellow?'

'I'd sure like to think so, ma'am. Thanks for the coffee. You've been a great help and comfort.'

'Comfort?' she said quizzically, looking him in the eye. 'Well, if you're sure. It was nice meeting you Mr . . . Mr. . . .' She'd forgotten his name already.

Jacob took his leave, mounted up and was just turning the horse when. . . .

'I say there, sonny! Young man,' she called, waving her hand at him. 'This was in the box, so might be sumpin' to do with it.' She came over to the gate and handed Jacob a deck of playing-cards. He looked at it. Was she completely crazy? She poked her finger at the deck.

'I remember now,' she said, wagging her finger. 'Hal was sure they wouldn't go looking in there. Take it if you want, it's no use to me.'

Jacob smiled, not meaning to be condescending; he thanked her again, slipped the deck of cards into his coat pocket, then pressed his heels into the side of the horse.

The sun was fast disappearing behind the mountain range when Jacob wearily rode into the livery corral and slid down from the saddle. Knowing that he would soon need his own horse, he enquired about a reputable dealer and, given a name, noted it as a priority.

Rachel was still in the shop premises as he walked past on his way to the hotel. He went in.

'Still here? I thought you would have finished for the day.'

'So much to do,' she replied. 'Even with the bits of furniture they left upstairs it's going to be at least another three or four days before we can move in here. I didn't think you were coming back until tomorrow.'

'I was lucky. I managed to conclude business sooner than I expected.'

No more was said on the subject. Rachel enquired no further and Jacob divulged nothing else. He was pleased she had enough to be getting on with. He would tell her more when the time was right.

'Which fabric for the curtains?' she wondered.

'It's up to you, Rachel. You're mistress of the house, you decide. Winters here will be cold. You'll need to line them to keep out the draughts.'

Jacob knew he could trust his sister to make a comfortable home. He wasn't uninterested, but there were more urgent matters on his mind, one of which was to arrange the next shipment. By the time they were set up with sufficient local interest Clifford would be displaying the fall fashions in Chicago. It would be a sure-fire winner to have similar lines from the East on show in a remote outpost like Beckinson.

Old Beckinson was almost obliterated by new buildings which had sprung up in the last few years. Although well away from the heart of the new mining country, it was not far from the gateway of burgeoning towns on the edge of the Rocky Mountains. Beckinson was ripe for development: the first stopping-off point for the steady flow of prospectors and their many needs, and just a day's stage journey out of Denver, where the tourist trade was growing. Foundations had already been laid for Beckinson's third hotel, boldly advertised on a billboard as the new Sandford Palace. It was going to be bigger than the two existing hotels put together. There was clearly the hope that business would boom.

A few days of hard graft had brought the refitting of Jacob and Rachel's store to completion. The exterior weatherboard had a new coat of paint. New signage had been erected announcing:

## J & R BURLEN of CHICAGO.
### High Class Outfitters, Haberdashery and Millinery.

The premises were attracting a lot of attention, and no lady had yet passed by without glancing to see when the grand opening was due.

Inside the shop the shelving was finished and painted. A large mahogany cutting table with an inlaid brass ruler along one side stood at the back of the shop, and a display counter had been constructed on Jacob's side. Rachel had acquired the unwanted cabinets from the shop that had been moving to Denver, and new hat stands had been made from painted pine. Mirrors were screwed to the walls, and fine brocade-upholstered chairs for customers had arrived from Denver.

Jacob, Rachel and three local girls, hired as shop helpers and seamstresses, had made splendid displays of their stock. Upstairs, a cleaning company had refreshed the living quarters. The previous owners had left some unwanted furniture which would do for the moment. Rachel made Jacob promise they'd go to Denver for new furniture as soon as the business became profitable.

Later that evening, after Rachel had gone to bed, Jacob was sitting at a table looking at the deck of cards. He recalled widow Hart's words: *Hal said they wouldn't go looking in there.* So what was in there? He could see nothing. Looking at the ornate ace of pades with its eagle and fancy foliage, it was an ordinary *Excelsior* deck by Dougherty of New York. Were names hidden in the cards? Black ink on black cards, maybe. That meant clubs or spades.

He looked again and sure enough, on each card in the suit of spades were some very small neat letters written to either side of the little stem on the spade pips, so small as to be easily missed. After a few moments of deciphering, the nine pip cards revealed nine names. Three more names were hidden on each of the three court cards; one was a dreadful shock. That made twelve names. Then, as he looked again at the ace of spades, he saw, cleverly disguised within the decorative foliage surrounding the large central spade symbol, the two names so cruelly etched into his mind.

So that was it. Twelve jurors on the two to the king, and the two most guilty men on the ace. God bless you, Hal Hart!

Jacob committed the names to memory while planning his next moves. Tomorrow he would get a new deck and write the names clearly on each of the spades. Then he would take a closer look at the new church and, more particularly, at the old cemetery.

**6**

A fresh morning breeze was stirring the Main Street dust. Jacob pulled his hat down over his eyes, and strode along the boardwalk in the direction of the church. The old timber building had accommodated most of the local population in a cramped mixture of chairs and pine pews. All that had gone now; a much grander structure was in its place. He wistfully remembered the creaking seats and the rustling of dresses as the women stood up and sat down. Then there had also been the special way the old pastor paused when people sat down. There was a moment of settled silence before he spoke. When he did, it was to tell stories of people in hot, dusty, faraway lands who trekked through deserts, fished in lakes and listened to prophets.

Jacob had always followed the pastor's stories with great interest, especially the one about Joseph, whose brightly coloured coat had caused his brothers' envy, and led to him being dumped in a well and sold to nomads. Poor Joseph, taken away from his family, kidnapped and forgotten, growing up without parents, wrongfully accused by a rebuffed woman, and facing death in prison. But it all came good in the end. He saved the people from starvation, became the pharaoh's right-hand man and even forgave his brothers. How emotional must have been that meeting with his frail old father after all those years, the father who loved him best of all but had been tricked into thinking he was dead. How had Joseph found it in himself to forgive brothers who had done all that?

Sadly, for Jacob Burlen there would be no emotional reunion with his father, nor with his mother. It was not he who had been kidnapped, but they who had been taken away from *him*. How was he supposed to find forgiveness for the people who had done that?

'Pastor Creeley?' Jacob called out, on seeing the minister shuffling towards the church gate.

The pastor turned round to see who had summoned him.

'Good day to you, sir,' he replied in a shaky voice so much weaker than Jacob remembered. The pastor, even more aged, white-haired and walking with a stoop, opened the gate in the picket fence. They went through together into the churchyard.

'I'm Jacob Burlen, the owner of the new haberdashery shop on Main Street.'

'Ah, yes. Mr Burlen and your pretty young wife—'

'Rachel's my sister.'

'Forgive me,' said the pastor, raising both hands at his clumsy mistake; it was one forgiveness that Jacob could easily bestow.

They reached the church door and the pastor opened it, stepping aside to let Jacob pass through.

'Such a fine building,' Jacob declared, admiring the vaulted roof and the large arched windows with their delicate wooden tracery.

'Raised on public subscription,' the pastor proclaimed proudly. 'The very generous gift of the local people and especially of our two benefactors, the proprietors of the town bank. Have you met Mr Sandford and Mr Martin? They take a keen interest in the local businesses and in encouraging commercial activity.'

Jacob dared not say yes, but then in all honesty he couldn't say no either.

'They haven't yet called in to see us,' he said truthfully.

'They will, I'm sure,' the pastor asserted with a broad toothy smile, the corners of his mouth damp with spittle. 'Such an asset to a town to have such generous founding fathers. Mr Sandford's the mayor, you know.'

'Founding fathers?' Jacob said quizzically, finding the emotive epithet a little strong. The pastor looked quite surprised.

'Why yes, indeed. Had you been here some ten years ago you'd have seen a little frontier town struggling to survive. The only trade was in beef and horses. The street was a sea of mud for half the year, the boardwalks were badly built, even some of the commercial premises were only fit to be pulled down, and of course the church was just a small cramped building without even enough furniture for all the folk to sit down.' He paused and made a show of looking round the spacious interior, sweeping his arm round in a gesture of delight. 'And look at it now.'

Jacob said nothing; he didn't want to interrupt the flow of information which the minister was exuberantly divulging.

'Then suddenly it all changed, just as if the town had found a crock of gold. New buildings started to spring up, the sheriff's office was pulled down and a grand new one built in its place. A bank was opened and money was freely lent to worthy citizens being encouraged to invest in the town's future. Enterprises of all sorts were begun: a lumber yard, new livery stables, a regular stage to Denver, and then, of course, the talk of rich veins of silver in the mountains.'

'For a priest you certainly know a lot about the commercial dealings in this town,' Jacob observed. 'I thought God and Mammon were on opposite sides.'

The priest turned a pair of tired, grey eyes on Jacob.

'I would have said the same in my younger days, Mr Burlen. Maybe people in the East with high ideals and comfortable living can afford to separate spiritual needs from financial ones. In the West you'll find us a deal more down to earth. Body and soul can only be kept together with one eye on God and the other on the Devil.'

'I'll keep that in mind, Pastor Creeley. Do you mind if I take a walk round the outside?'

'The church is a physical place for contemplation Mr Burlen, inside and outside. Just as a man is a vessel of God, inside and outside.'

'Well, thank you for your time; it's been uplifting.'

They shook hands and Jacob went out into the warm summer sunshine. It was only then that it struck him how cold it had been inside the lofty structure. The pastor was clearly a great supporter of the church's benefactors. Had Sandford and Martin really become such good citizens?

The cemetery was marked out in plots, the oldest part going back twenty-five years or more when there had been no more than a handful of inhabitants. They were hardy folk, prepared to fight off Indians, harsh winters and poor harvests to build their little community into the beginnings of a town. Their graves were marked by wooden crosses and neat stones. As the town grew so the wooden crosses gave way to roughly cut headstones, and as prosperity increased so did the carvings on the tombstones.

Jacob moved slowly through the neat rows, looking to the right and left. The numbers of citizens who passed away each year must have increased as the town grew. Almost untouched by the Civil War, the settlement had blossomed after Johnny Reb was put down and Southern discontents and Union entrepreneurs started moving westwards.

Jacob suddenly stopped stock still; his heart missed a beat. He fell down on one knee and took off his hat. How strange it was to see those names chiselled into the hard cold stone. Zachary Peterson and his wife, Rebecca. The words were painted in black letters, partly fading, noting simply that they were citizens of the town, and they had both died in 1866: *I am the resurrection and the life. He that believeth in me, though he were dead, yet shall he live. St John chap 11.*

Someone must have paid for this headstone; Jacob wondered who that might have been. He stood up and bowed his head, holding his hat with both hands and muttered the Lord's Prayer to himself, emphasizing: 'thy *will* be done'. As he said 'Amen' he heard the church door being closed and he watched the black-cassock-clad figure shuffle down the path.

When Pastor Creeley turned to latch the gate he stood a moment and half-raised his right hand towards Jacob, then briefly made the sign of the cross as if blessing him. Jacob acknowledged with a wave and felt a pulse of optimism ripple through his body, turning melancholy into contentment. It was a strange feeling: a surge of warmth almost as if God himself was giving consent.

With renewed determination, Jacob now read the names very carefully of those who had died in the last ten years. He found five that now had significant meaning.

He spent the afternoon sorting fabrics and accessories. He barely noticed the patterns on the bolts, so recently packed with Clifford's help, hoping they would capture the imagination of the good townswomen of Beckinson. His mind was not fully on the task but he was nevertheless careful to separate the silks from the cottons and the woollens and the calicos, and to arrange the colours in an attractive order. There were also the rich brocades and plain velvets for furnishings, and simple linens, lawns and ticking for lining.

While sorting and shifting, Jacob was deep in thought,

not so much about the store in Chicago, a thousand miles away, but going back ten years in time, and wondering what had actually happened. Before he knew it, Rachel was standing quietly by his side.

'It's time we went back to the hotel, Jacob,' she said, taking one of his hands in both of hers. 'I've been watching you today. Sorting your fabrics while the girls were busy with the hat display and arranging my side of the shop.'

'*Your* side? That sounds very territorial,' Jacob said with a laugh.

'Well it is,' she replied smiling at him. 'That is definitely my side, and this is yours. Maybe we share the girls as helpers, but we'll see who makes the most profit in the first month.'

'You're so determined to outdo me.'

'Of course,' said Rachel, smiling. 'It's called sibling rivalry! But your mind was somewhere else today, I could tell you weren't concentrating.' She walked over to his shelves. 'Look, what's this pale-pink bolt of glazed silk doing in here with the printed cottons?'

Jacob acknowledged the mistake. 'You win!' he said. 'Let's go and get something to eat for dinner at the hotel.'

'I can't wait to move in here, a proper place of our own.'

Jacob nodded. 'A couple more days and I reckon it'll all be ready.'

After dinner, as they were sitting in their hotel suite, Rachel was reading a novel, one of several that Leila had recommended and which she had bought for Rachel in a Chicago bookshop. Jacob had opened his copy of the Bible at John's Gospel chapter eleven to find the quotation on their parents' headstone. He scanned through the verses: it was about a man called Lazarus and how Jesus brought him back to life: a puzzling story about who Jesus really was. Jacob had just got beyond verse twenty-eight, where Mary says *The Master is come and calleth for thee* when he heard a knock on the door.

Momentarily startled, he blurted out loud, 'For me?' He hoped Rachel hadn't noticed; quietly he closed the book and opened the door to find one of the hotel maids holding a letter.

'This has just come for you, sir, with a request that it be delivered at once.'

Jacob took the letter and thanked the maid. He slid his finger under the seal, opened the single sheet and began to read. It was a very brief letter.

'How very strange. What does it say? Who is it from?' Rachel asked, putting down her book and coming over to see.

Jacob hesitated; he held the letter close to his chest so that she might not see it.

'Erm – erm – nothing really. Just a note.'

'Come then, let me see it.' She held out her hand but when he wouldn't give the letter to her she tried to snatch it away.

'No secrets, Jacob. You mustn't have any secrets from me.'

He held it high in the air so that she might not reach it.

'It's not a secret, it's just a note.'

'Let me see it then,' she persisted.

He relented and gave it to her. She read it out loud:

'*We must meet as soon as you can. Come to the black tree at first light tomorrow.*' Rachel let her hands drop to her lap with the note. She looked to her brother. 'What does it mean, Jacob? Are you seeing a young lady already!'

'Of course not,' he replied indignantly. 'I'll just have to go and find out.'

' "*The black tree*". That sounds like something out of a dime novel. Do you know where it is?'

'I'm not sure. Look, I'm going down to the saloon for a drink. Do you mind?'

She smiled. 'Of course not. I'll probably go to bed soon anyway.'

Going down the stairs Jacob was ill at ease. He had been hoping that nobody would ever recognize them. Could somebody possibly know who he was? Maybe it had been a big mistake to come back to Beckinson, perhaps he should have set up in Denver and just travelled into Beckinson when he needed to. It was too late now. Of course, neither he not Rachel looked the same after ten years, they had just been children then; they had even had a different surname.

But somebody had guessed something.

In the hotel saloon, twisting the glass of whiskey round in his hand, he pondered on the day's events. Rachel had noticed he wasn't paying attention in the shop. It had been an emotional day, made worse because he was determined to keep things to himself. He would keep Rachel in the dark about his reason for coming to Beckinson. After all, she had been only five when they left for Chicago, and Beckinson had changed so much. He hoped she remembered nothing of the past. He hoped – but for himself – that the waiting, the planning, the searching was nearly over.

*Come to the black tree at first light tomorrow.* Who could know about that? It was time to set out on the path of retribution.

# 7

As the sun began to spread its light across the plains in the east Jacob pitched up at the livery and took a mount for the day. He had left Rachel sleeping peacefully in their hotel suite. Her day would be busy enough. They were hoping to vacate the hotel tomorrow and move in over the shop. Today she was going to make sure everything was ready. Mounting the livery's old quarter horse, he reminded himself to get a pair of horses once they moved in; the yard and outbuildings at the back of their premises would provide adequate stabling, and local people wouldn't so easily be able to follow his comings and goings.

*The black tree.* Only a few older residents of Beckinson would know the black tree. It was about two miles, maybe two-and-a-half miles, out of town. Jacob had known it because it was close to the boundary of his parents' ranch. A big old cottonwood that had been struck by lightning during a violent summer storm. It had lost a couple of big branches, ripped off by the strike that had set the tree ablaze, burning the whole thing from top to toe.

The lashing rain had eventually put the fire out but the bare tree was left standing, a ghostly shape and as black as the night. When he had been allowed to ride on his own his pa had always said: *no further than the black tree.* Who else would know about that?

Jacob left the main trail and rode down through the aspens and oaks until he came within sight of the old cottonwood on the far side of a clearing. Other trees had grown up around it but it stood there black, gaunt and foreboding with a pair of crows sitting on a naked branch. It was well off the beaten track and, approaching cautiously, Jacob slipped the gun out of his jacket and checked that all six chambers were loaded. He had no idea what he would do if he felt the need to defend himself, as he was completely inexperienced in the use of a handgun. He wasn't even sure why he'd brought the gun with him.

He pulled up his mount near the tree and slid down off the saddle. Should he have dismounted further away and watched to see who turned up? It was too late now; he was off the horse and a sitting duck for anyone with evil intentions. Maybe somebody else was already there and watching him from a distance. The crows flapped noisily off their perch, cawing their raucous call into the air. Something moved in the undergrowth, a deer perhaps? He looked round nervously. Then a voice called out.

'Jacob! It's all right, it's me, John.' The man emerged from the trees, sitting astride a horse. 'I'm so glad you've come.'

'John? But how. . . ?'

'Don't worry, your secret is safe with me. Pastor Creeley knew who you were as soon as he saw you saying a prayer by your parents' grave. He sent word to Abigail and me. We knew you'd be back one day. Mount up and follow me, Abi's got coffee on the go and a nice side of bacon sizzling in the pan.'

Jacob hadn't thought about breakfast until that moment but his mouth watered at the thought of some smoky bacon and eggs.

'Lead on,' he said cheerfully.

A mile or two of steady trotting brought them to a ranch.

A fine herd of beeves were munching in the fields and a welcome stream of smoke rose from the ranch-house chimney. Despite the good summer weather, a fire first thing in the morning was always welcome and a good sign that something tasty was cooking on the stove.

It was an emotional greeting. Jacob was transported back ten years as he hugged Abigail and remembered the enveloping warmth of her starched apron with its nose-tingling smell and the faint hint of roses that scented the air behind her wherever she went. She was older, of course, and her hair was full of grey wisps but her smile was as lovely as ever and her skin as soft as a newborn babe.

John looked little changed: a few more lines on his weather-beaten face and grey hair at his temples but otherwise the same stocky, sturdy ranch hand who had faithfully worked the Peterson spread. The smell of the bacon was beginning to be irresistible.

'So you didn't sell out to the Denver meat-packing company, like all the others?'

'No, we didn't,' John asserted vehemently. 'We bought this place after your . . . after your . . . when your parents passed away. A little while later, when Sandford and his sidekick, Clem Martin, started buying up all the ranches, we made it plain we weren't going to be bought out. Your pa's ranch was the first one they took, of course. That gave them access to the silver mine, the one at Devil's Leap.

'Now they own a bank, a silver mine, two hotels, half the town and almost everything else. We always expected you to come back, but not to live and certainly not to be setting up a shop. You've changed a lot and I can't say I would have recognized you if I'd passed you in the street.'

'Well, the pair of you have hardly changed at all,' Jacob said. 'I did wonder if we would run into each other, or if I would still recognize you, but I didn't know whether you had stayed in Beckinson or not.'

'We nearly didn't,' Abigail said, turning the bacon over in the pan and cracking some eggs. 'We nearly didn't.'

John began to explain. 'What happened to your pa was bad enough, but when your mother too. . . .'

Jacob looked down. 'How did that happen? I heard she was found in the river.'

John was silent, Abigail turned the food on to plates and set them on the table. She looked Jacob in the eye sympathetically.

'She never properly regained her senses. After they hanged your pa – God rest his soul and may his accusers rot in hell – she started to wander around the town seemingly in a daze. Ambrose Sandford kept pestering her and – well – we think he tried to . . . you know, force himself on her, poor woman. One day she just walked into the river, went right on walking and that was that.'

'On purpose, you think?'

Abigail shook her head.

'Can't say, Jacob; we were looking after you and Rachel. Your ma's mind wasn't right with everything an' all. She couldn't focus herself on anything. *Always* in a daze, a soul in torment. She couldn't believe what they done to your pa, him being such a good, gentle husband. The things they said about him.' She sucked in a noisy breath and wanted to change the subject. 'And how is Rachel? Will you bring her out to see us?'

'I will,' said Jacob. 'I will, when the time is right. We're moving into the shop tomorrow. Come and see us, but not yet, and please don't let on that you know us. Rachel is not yet ready to hear about those things. She was only five as you know, and I don't want her to be thinking on anything else except the shop right now.'

When he had finished breakfast and chatting Jacob took his leave of his two faithful kindly old guardians. Before he mounted up, he turned to John.

'You see I'm not wearing a gunbelt,' Jacob said.

'Yes, I noticed that.'

'But I've got a gun, here in my pocket. The truth is I don't rightly know how to shoot the wretched thing. Do you think you might give me some lessons?'

'You come out here any time you like and I'll teach you,' John replied, helping himself to the Schofield. He turned it over in his hand and levelled it to feel the balance. 'It's a mighty fine piece. Make a pretty big hole in someone with that. Is that why you've come back now?'

'Maybe,' Jacob said, and left it at that.

'Take care,' John admonished. 'I guess you've come for Sandford and Martin. Clem Martin always was a bad lot and he ain't improved none.'

'There's others I've got to see before I have to worry about him or Sandford.'

'Sandford has a lot of friends in Beckinson, not least of which is Curtis O'Donnel.'

'The sheriff?'

'And most of the deputies. They're all on Sandford's payroll. Sandford's the mayor.'

'Yes, I heard.'

'He's a crooked sonofabitch, pretending to be a great philanthropist and benefactor. Don't trust anyone, Jacob, there were a lot of pay-outs ten years ago. People don't forget that kinda generosity.'

'Why did they pick on my pa?' Jacob asked, his voice beginning to crack with emotion.

'I guess they needed a fall guy for the murder of Clem's brother Tod, so Clem could inherit the silver mine. Sandford had a grudge against your pa. We all knew he wanted your ma for his wife. It all came together one drunken night in a storm. They did the beating and the shooting. Then Sandford never stopped pestering your ma after . . . you know.'

'Well, it's time for another pay-out,' Jacob said. He heeled his horse into a sudden trot so that John wouldn't see the tears pricking at his eyes.

Jacob and Rachel Burlen had been living in their new home for just three days. It was beginning to look exactly like Rachel had imagined. The paintwork still smelled fresh and the pine floorboards had the strong aroma of wax polish. She would, however, be glad when they could afford new furniture.

'And when we can,' she said emphatically, 'we'll take the stage into Denver and choose the very best we can buy.'

'First things first, Rachel. The grand opening is in two days' time and we've got to have everything just so. Ret Murphy at the newspaper office has promised to have a photographer in attendance and to put the pictures in the window and in the *Clarion*. Which reminds me, I have to see Ret and pick up the discount vouchers he's printed for us.'

Their new maid, Anna, had lit a fire and coffee was on the stove.

'Do we have any of that steak left, Anna?'

'Yes sir, we do. With eggs?'

'And a bucket of hot coffee,' he replied.

Anna had been a lucky find; Jacob hadn't even had to advertise for anyone: she just turned up one morning at the shop, stepped right in and asked Rachel if they had any work. She was probably about Jacob's age; they didn't ask her exactly. Her skin was a rich olive colour, her hair was glossy black and her high cheekbones suggested there was some Indian ancestry in her. She was a fine cook, which Jacob made her demonstrate before taking her on, but what clinched the deal was that she had a brother, three or four years younger, who was good with horses.

So they took them both on: Anna and Ruan, she as a

maid and home help, Ruan as a stable lad and handy boy, though Jacob told him not wear the belly-gun that he seemed to carry all the time, stuffed into his belt.

'Just a habit,' Ruan had said. 'Pa told me always to take care of my sister.'

There was a good solid shed in the yard for them to live in. Anna cleaned it out top to toe and polished the wood-work. Ruan painted everything else. Rachel ran up some curtains and a tablecloth and Jacob bought just enough fur-niture from a local carpenter for them to be reasonably comfortable. Everyone was happy.

While Anna was fixing breakfast Jacob went downstairs and out into the yard.

'Ruan?'

Ruan poked his head out of the stable, which housed the two good workaday horses that Jacob had finally got round to buying.

'Ah, there you are,' said Jacob. 'I want you to saddle up my horse.'

'Yes, Mr Burlen; do you want saddlebags and a pack strapped on?'

'No, just have the horse saddled, nothing extra. I'll be down as soon as I've had breakfast.'

Jacob breathed in the fresh warm summer air and felt well pleased with himself. Clifford would be proud of him. The shop was nearly open, the accommodation was fin-ished, they had a maid and a lad and everything was good. There was still much to do, and not just for the shop. He had made another trip out to see John and already felt more at ease holding the Schofield, though his aim was still pretty poor.

At least he wasn't afraid to squeeze the trigger. There were plenty of people carrying guns in Beckinson. This part of the West was a long way from the civilization of Chicago. However, he never wanted to be seen wearing a gun. He stopped daydreaming and went back upstairs, two at a time, in an ebullient mood, ready for a hearty breakfast.

Before going to see Ret Murphy at the *Clarion*, Jacob rode out to John and Abigail's ranch. With all the excitement of moving into their new home Rachel's curiosity about the black tree and his early-morning meeting had thankfully been forgotten. As he rode into the ranch yard Jacob could see that John had a row of tin cans at the ready and a box of shells. They walked out to a small coppice from where the noise wouldn't disturb Abigail. It was with some shame that, after working his way through fifty bullets, Jacob could see the tin cans were still pretty much intact. There had been less than a handful of direct hits, and those were more by luck than judgement.

'You're getting better,' John said encouragingly. 'And I did increase the distance a bit. Now listen, aim for that can in the middle. Bring your gun up slowly, arm's length, feet steady, knees soft; relax your arm, take up the tension on the trigger and breathe out as you squeeze it. Squeeze!'

There was a loud retort as another piece of hot lead flew past the cans and into the woods.

'Go again, and this time pause just above the tin, then lower your gun a fraction and fire.'

Another loud bang, another piece of lead, another miss.

'That's better,' John exclaimed.

'How on earth can you tell that?'

'Trust me. Now pause again with your aim just above the tin. This time when you fire try to bring the gun back to exactly the same place just above the can and hold it there as soon as you pull the trigger. Keep your elbow soft.'

Bang! The can flew up into the air and Jacob let out a whoop of delight at his success. John handed him another box of shells.

'Now I'm going to leave you with this lot. Concentrate, take them all down, stand them up and take them down again and again until they're all as holey as a honeycomb. When you've done, come in and have a drink.'

For a moment Jacob hesitated; he wondered why he was doing this. In his heart he knew he could never look into somebody's eye and pull the trigger, hoping to kill them. This was a charade. He was more comfortable in the shop serving customers, more comfortable talking about fabrics and finishes, about buttons and lace, ribbons, the fashions from Paris. The whole venture began to feel like a gigantic mistake. What had started out as a distant dream of revenge had become a nightmare of obligation; a task he had set himself but which he began to doubt he could even begin, let alone complete. Ten years is a long time. A time to forget, to let wounds heal.

Staring into the distance without looking, Jacob hadn't felt himself tensing under the pressure of indecision until suddenly he startled himself by unwittingly pulling the trigger. The bullet ripped into the ground inches away from his foot, throwing up small stones and a cloud of dust. Instinctively he leapt back. The leap was not just in distance but in time as well. The acrid smoke and unexpected noise took him back to the knothole in the bedroom wall and the bullet that Ambrose Sandford fired at point-blank range into Tod Martin's chest. He could almost feel the vibration in the floorboards again.

Holding the gun at arm's length, Jacob fired off the entire box of shells, in between running backwards and forwards to stand the five cans up again and again. Three of them were by now so shot to pieces they could barely be stood up. He was in a state of high excitement when he joined John in a glass of whiskey at the kitchen table. John had a twinkle in his eye.

'You're looking mighty pleased with yourself. I said you were getting better. You didn't know how I could tell, but I could. You used to shoot real good with that ol' Spencer

your pa had. You always had a good eye: all I had to show
you was a little trick to give you back your confidence.
That's all it is, you know, confidence.'

Jacob wanted to say that it wasn't just confidence, especially as he didn't feel he had too much of that. But what he
realized he did have – by the bucketful – was anger.
Vengefulness was what had just put all those holes in the tin
cans. Vengefulness and anger might just give him enough
confidence to do what he knew he couldn't avoid.

**8**

Riding back into town Jacob couldn't decide whether he really did feel better or not. Sure, he'd shot some holes in a few tin cans. He knew his eye was good and his hand steady; after all you can't measure and cut fabric with a pair of shears without coordinated hand and eye. A pair of shears and a gun – a rifle especially, the way you hold them is strikingly similar. The movement to reload a rifle is the same as a cut with the shears. The hand movements are the same. He remembered how he used to reload his pa's Spencer; perhaps that was why he had found it so easy to cut with shears. When Clifford had first handed him a pair to see if he could follow a straight line, he declared Jacob a natural haberdasher. Could he be a natural gunslinger too?

He hitched outside the offices of the *Beckinson Clarion* and went in to see Ret Murphy. Ret was watching one of the presses. He turned round at the sound of the swinging door bell.

'Mr Jacob Burlen. Good morning. Ready for your grand opening?'

Ret Murphy was a young man in his late twenties, maybe early thirties, but already wearing thick glasses. His hair was receding where it had been worn away by the eyeshade. With that and the slight stoop characteristic of all printers who spend long hours bent over the compositing table, he looked a good deal older than his years.

'Your shop vouchers are ready,' he said, pointing to them on the shelf. 'Do you want to take them now?'

'Yup, I'll take them,' Jacob said. 'Send the invoice across to the shop when it's ready. By the way, do you have old copies of the *Clarion* stored away somewhere?'

'We certainly do,' Ret assured him, 'every goddam copy ever printed. 'Course, I've only been here since '72 but there's a complete archive upstairs. Do you want to take a look?'

'Would you mind?'

'This way.' Ret showed Jacob through the office to the back stairs. 'Anything in particular?'

'No, just curious.'

Ret laughed. 'They say curiosity killed the cat, you know,'

'Yes, I've heard,' Jacob said, matter of fact. Ret pushed a door open and pointed to the boxes stacked along the wall.

'It starts here, and so far as I can tell they're in order. The first issue was in 1865 at the end of the war, when new people were settling in the area for prospecting and ranching. Just a simple one-fold news sheet published whenever there was enough news. Then as the town grew so did the paper, right up to today's weekly four-fold paper. Anyway, make yourself at home, and please put them all back in the right order, or I'll come over and muddle up your fabrics! I must get back to the press.'

Jacob looked in the first box. The papers had been thin when the publication started, the typeface was all different sizes and the page looked a bit of a jumble. He only had to go as far as the second box to find the run for 1866. It didn't take long to find what he was looking for: the details of the trial of Zachary Peterson, accused of the murder of Tod Martin.

The events were reported in three issues. Jacob read part-way through the first report. Then he let the news sheet drop to his lap. He had to face a difficult decision. It was time to tell Rachel why they had come to Beckinson.

The newspapers would give him the courage to start what was going to be a difficult conversation. He lifted out the three copies and went downstairs.

'Ret, I'd like to borrow these three. I'll bring them back tomorrow.'

'Sure you can. Don't forget your vouchers,' Ret said.

Jacob took the old newspapers and the vouchers. He walked along the street to the shop and sent Ruan back to fetch his horse. Rachel was busy with the girls putting the finishing touches to the shop displays. When the wall clock struck five they all stopped work for the day and stepped back to admire the result.

'What do you think, Jacob?'

'Wonderful,' he said. 'You've all worked so hard. We've brought a little bit of Chicago out west to Beckinson. A little bit of Paris too.'

The counters and the shelves were elaborately festooned with ribbon, braids and tassels for the grand opening. Rachel's window to the right of the entrance was filled with a display of fine hats for ladies. It had attracted attention all through the day. Simple bonnets were placed towards the back, fancy bonnets at the front with their ribbons and lace trimmings. To the right were the fine fashions with feathers, gauze and trimmings. There was something to suit all pockets and all tastes.

In Jacob's window three large mannequins were dressed in the finest fabrics from Chicago. On the left was a stylish dress made of pale-pink silk and deep-red velvet, the silk hanging in folds over a pleated skirt with velvet bands. In the centre an ornate affair with a bustle and train would surprise the Beckinson ladies, but it was worn almost as an everyday garment by some of the wealthier women in the East. Lastly, there was a beautiful sleeveless flounced décolleté evening dress in two shades of blue taffeta and watered silk. All three had caused a stir as they were being assembled. The town was clearly buzzing with expectation.

After dinner Jacob and Rachel were sitting by the fire. Anna had finished clearing up and they were now alone for the evening. Rachel as usual was engrossed in her novel but Jacob couldn't settle. The newspapers were on his mind. He didn't know where to begin. At length he stood up.

'The black tree,' he said.

'Oh, yes, the black tree,' Rachel repeated, putting her book down. 'What a mystery! I've been so busy with the shop I forgot to ask. Was it a young lady?' she enquired mischievously.

'I haven't been quite honest with you, Rachel. I wanted to protect you from things that you've probably forgotten, or maybe never really knew. Now that we're ready to open the shop and you'll meet lots of local people there are things which you have to know.'

'What sort of things?' she asked, intrigued.

'About our parents, and that sort of thing.'

Her brow furrowed. 'I thought they were dead.'

'They are.'

'They were killed in an accident. Aunt Leila told me so.'

'Killed yes, but not in any accident,' Jacob corrected.

Rachel didn't respond for a moment, she looked at Jacob quizzically.

'Not an accident?'

Jacob heaved a huge sigh as if he was unburdening a great weight.

'I don't know where to begin, really. Does the name Abigail mean anything to you?'

'Abigail? Yes, I've heard that name. Didn't we use to know someone. . . .'

'Perhaps that's where I should start.'

Jacob related the whole sad story of how the night of the storm started off a chain of events which spiralled out of all reason and ended so tragically with the hanging of their father and the drowning of their mother. He kept his composure as best he could while telling Rachel how they were taken in and looked after by John and Abigail, and why they had later been adopted by their relatives in Chicago.

Rachel listened with her head held high while tears flowed down her cheeks. Never once did she try to hide them or brush them aside. It was typical Rachel: if there was a bridge to be crossed she would always meet it square on, never looking for a way back or a softer option. She knew that whatever had to be faced in life was best met eye to eye, tears and all. Perhaps those traumatic days had affected them more deeply than either of them had ever understood.

'I always knew there was something,' she said, 'something I couldn't quite remember. Something dark, something not quite right.'

'Now I'm not sure if I've done the right thing,' Jacob admitted.

'I had to know,' Rachel reassured him.

'No, not about telling you, I mean in coming back to Beckinson.'

'I don't know, Jacob. What are you planning to do? You must be planning something or you wouldn't have brought us here.'

He felt honour-bound to tell Rachel what he had been doing.

'I found the widow of the old sheriff, Hal Hart, and paid her a visit. Well, I didn't know Sheriff Hart was dead; anyway we had a long chat and she gave me a deck of cards which had names hidden on them. Names of the twelve men who lied under oath and sent our pa to the gallows. Sheriff Hart knew what they were doing, but couldn't do anything to stop it. Five of the jurymen are dead now, buried in the churchyard. That leaves seven. One of them lives out on the road to Denver. His name was on a board at the gate to his house. I recognized the name, Pilotski, because I remember seeing it on a poster while we were in Denver; an unusual name, unless it's a very odd coincidence. He's wanted for murder: killed a woman bystander in the process of a violent robbery.'

But Rachel could see beyond that one man; instinct told her there was more to it.

'And when you find all these people? What then?'

Jacob sighed. 'I don't know. That's just what I don't know.'

Rachel suddenly looked aghast. 'You're not thinking of killing them?'

'Why not?'

'It would be murder.'

'What's the difference? That's exactly what they did to our pa. And our ma, kind of.'

Rachel held her hand up. ' "*Vengeance is mine saith the Lord*". You know that's what it says in the Bible, it's in one of St Paul's letters, I think. We were told it often enough in Sunday school. People do things for their own reasons and they have to account for it on the Day of Judgment before the Lord.'

'But a commandment says to honour your father and mother.'

'And the very next one says "*thou shalt not kill*",' Rachel countered.

'But they did.' There was a momentary pause. 'So we just let them get away with it?'

'Or go to the sheriff.'

Jacob shook his head. 'No, we can't do that. He's on the payroll.'

'Tell me, Jacob, did you think we were coming back here so you could just kill all these people? Some of them may have families, children. Think of that. What would Leila and Clifford say if they knew about this?'

Jacob threw his hands up in the air.

'All right, Sis. You're a right-minded person, you're fair and kind and forgiving. But people who act outside the law

75

are exactly what will bring this country down. Decent honest people, like our parents, can't prosper in a country where lawless people do just whatever they like. You can't go around disregarding the law, lying under oath, condemning innocent people.

'There's always greed at the heart of everything, people wanting something they can't have, or wanting to take what someone else has got. Greed and envy. That's what took away our parents, their lives, our lives. Did they deserve that? Did we?'

'No, but—'

Jacob cut her short. 'I'm sorry, Rachel, you're wrong about this. Do you think I can hold my head up high amongst these people knowing that somewhere here amongst them are liars who sent our pa to the gallows, caused our ma to walk into the river and never look back? Can you imagine that? They'll have to confess on the Day of Judgment, I know that, but so will I.

'Am I to say to St Peter, I was too weak to put right a dreadful act of wrong-doing, too yellow to be an honest, upright citizen, too scared to confront evil people? Well I'm prepared to let God be the judge of that. I'll let *him* decide whether I'm right or wrong.' He paused, exhausted by his own defiance, waiting for Rachel to say something, but she had nothing to say.

She simply looked up at him standing there with his eyes blazing and his hands shaking. He was her brother and she loved him, even in the face of the fire that burned in him right now, a dreadful fire that filled her with fear, the fear of losing him, carried away by inexperience and a terrible zeal. Walking like their ma into a river whose depth he couldn't possibly know. But did she really want him to be like St Peter, who, when brought to the test denied everything, turned his back and hid himself? Did she really want Jacob to be like that? The brother she had always looked up to, the one who had always protected her.

Jacob took a deep breath and was now perfectly calm.

'You can go back to Chicago if you want. I'll put you on the next train if you say so. You know Clifford and Leila wouldn't be disappointed in any way. You could open up another shop in Chicago perhaps. Your own little millinery shop across the other side of town.'

'Stop it! Stop it!' she cried, putting her hands over her ears and dissolving into sobs. 'I don't want to go away. My place is by your side, you know that. What we do we must do together.' Her shoulders were shaking with the convulsions. Jacob sat down beside her and put his arm round her.

'Rachel, Rachey, dearest Sis, I didn't want to upset you. But I had to tell you about these things.'

'I know,' she said, brushing the tears aside and taking her handkerchief out of her sleeve to dry her eyes. 'I know. And you know I wouldn't leave you to face this on your own. Perhaps you're right. Big brothers are supposed to be right, aren't they? I do trust you, Jacob. Promise me you'll be careful.'

He nodded and gave her a tender, brotherly hug. Rachel dabbed at her eyes, picked up her book and continued reading where she had left off. Jacob took up the three newspapers that he had borrowed from Ret Murphy and began to read the reports of the trial. The room was silent. It was as if everything that ever needed to be said on the matter had been said and finished. Five minutes later Rachel closed her book and went to bed. She bade Jacob good night. He waited a while then put down the newspapers and went to his room.

He opened the wardrobe and took out a high-collared, long coat made by himself of black velvet and lined with black silk. He took the Schofield and slipped it into a pocket which he had specially designed. He slipped silently out of the back door, crossed the yard and quietly opened and closed the gate. The night was quite still, the moon shone brightly in the clear starry sky, but the shadows allowed him to move quickly from darkness to darkness. The low hoot of a disturbed screech owl was the only commonplace advertisement of his presence.

Coming by and by to the little house out on the Denver road, he crept all the way round beneath each of the windows, pausing to listen for any movement. His heart was pounding. There was no light in any of the windows but one was slightly open. He eased it back and lifted himself inside. He stood for a moment to accustom his eyes. Moonlight came in through a gap in the shutter. He was in a single open space with a couple of sticks of furniture and a big empty tub in front of a fireplace.

For a moment Jacob lost all confidence. The fear of a mistake, the horror of freezing at the crucial moment, the doubt about his justification and, overriding everything, the fear of failure. Beads of sweat began to appear on his forehead. There was just one internal door, at the back of the room.

Jacob swallowed, then moved quietly towards it. Whereas his heart had been quietly pounding before, it was now thumping so loudly he was sure it would wake the occupant of the bedroom. He felt for the Schofield and eased it slowly into his hand. He flexed his fingers and felt the sweat on his palm. The latch on the door rose as he pressed down on the lever. It suddenly clicked too loudly: it was too late to turn back now so he pushed the door and went straight in, going as close to the bed's headboard as he could and flattening himself against the wall.

'What, wha. . . ?'

Jacob heard the man fumbling for something under the bed. Then, as he expected, a blast was fired in the direction of the door. A match was struck and held in a shaking hand towards a candle, which took light and slowly lit up the room. For a moment the man didn't see Jacob in the shadow so close to the bed.

Jacob moved quickly and pinned the man down on his bed with a knee on his chest; he pulled back the Schofield's hammer and pressed the gun into the man's forehead. The man threw up his hands.

'Whoa,' he said, 'you've got the wrong man. I ain't done nothin'. Who are you anyway? What's this all about?'

Jacob said nothing. He grabbed the man's right arm and, surprised by his own strength, held the man's hand back against the wall.

'Pilotski, you once raised your right hand, and swore a lying oath.'

He pressed the gun against Pilotski's palm and pulled the trigger. The room filled with acrid smoke and an ear-splitting noise. The man screamed in shock, terror and disbelief. Jacob let the man's arm flop on to the bed.

'That lie sent an innocent man to the gallows; that makes you a lying murderer. And I guess you're the same man as committed the armed robbery and took another innocent life in Denver.'

'What of it? She was unlucky,' Pilotski gasped, still shaking with painful surprise.

'And so are you,' said Jacob.

He pulled out the pillow from under the man's head and held it over his face. He leant back and at arm's length fired a single shot. The body instantly arched, then went limp as feathers and blood exploded into the air.

Jacob found himself panting, his mouth was dry, he ran his tongue round his lips. What was done was done, there was no going back now. He slipped his hand inside his coat and pulled out the six of spades. He tucked it inside the man's night-shirt.

'God forgive you,' he said. 'I don't.'

He blew out the candle, opened the bedroom window and disappeared silently into the darkness.

# 9

The day of the grand opening arrived at last. The sun shone and the townsfolk turned out in great numbers. Randall Tarne, deputy mayor and bank manager, cut the ribbon and made a short formal speech of welcome in front of the shop, which looked stunningly attractive. The three shop girls brought out trays of cookies and glasses of champagne. The wine had only just turned up at the last minute on the stage from Denver and had cost Jacob a pretty penny.

Jacob and Rachel circulated amongst the well-wishers and for the first time felt themselves to be a proper part of the town. It was a swell gathering and, when the formalities were over, most of the women filed into the store while the men dispersed to the town's saloons or back to their work.

True to his word Jacob called for Barbara, the wife of the land agent Dexter Gray, to come forward as she was to be his first official customer. He opened the ladies' fashion magazine that lay on the counter, to give her some ideas. Delighted she began to flick through its pages and was soon joined by a number of her friends who were very free with their advice.

On the other side of the shop Amelia Tarne, the bank manager's wife, was to be Rachel's first official customer, as Jacob had also promised, and she was seen trying on a variety of gaily coloured bonnets, turning her head from side to side in front of one of the gilt-framed mirrors.

The bell on the till was soon ringing as the customers started to spend their dollars. Several accounts were opened on the first day of trading and discount vouchers were distributed. When the shop girls were ready to go home Jacob and Rachel thanked them profusely for their part in the day's great success and gave them each a generous five-dollar bonus from the takings.

That evening Anna cooked a delicious beef stew with parsley, peas and turnips and a freshly baked round of corn bread. As it was a special occasion, Anna and Ruan joined them for the evening meal. Jacob opened a bottle of fine French wine that had come up with the case of champagne from Denver. True, it was only the first day of trading but the enthusiastic reception by the local people promised well for the future.

Before eating, Jacob stood up and raised his glass.

'To Clifford and Leila Burlen of Chicago, Jacob and Rachel Burlen of Beckinson, Anna and Ruan our trusty helpers, the good people of Beckinson, and the Union of American States!' They all raised their glasses and drank a toast.

While they were laughing and chatting, a knocking came from downstairs. Jacob pulled his pocket watch from his waistcoat and flipped the cover.

'Who the devil? At this time of night. Excuse me, please.'

He got up and went down the stairs, peering cautiously at the front double doors. There was no sign of anyone. Then another knock came from the back door.

'Hello,' he said, 'who's there?'

'A friend,' came the reply.

Jacob pulled back the bolt and opened the door a fraction; two men were standing on the step.

'Mr Burlen, we were hoping you and your sister would be

81

coming across to the saloon this evening for a celebratory drink.'

'Oh?' Jacob said.

'Mr Martin wanted to properly welcome you to Beckinson, it being your first day of trading an' all.'

'Really? He didn't come to the opening though. Anyway, that's mighty kind, but. . . .'

'Well, don't disappoint him. He don't take too well to disappointment.'

'Look it's quite late, we're just finishing dinner—'

'We'll tell him you'll be over shortly.' As they walked away to the yard gate, one looked back over his shoulder. 'Soon as you can,' he said.

Jacob closed the door. There could only be one Mr Martin, surely: Clem Martin – and he really did need to meet him, but not for a drink, not for a social visit. Yet they hadn't left him much choice; it would be bad manners not to accept the hospitality of one of the most influential men in Beckinson. Indeed it might be quite the wrong thing for business to snub such a man. He would have to go and meet him in the saloon. But without Rachel.

He went back upstairs and explained what had happened. He left the others to enjoy the last of the wine and the cheese while he tidied himself up. He walked across to the saloon and was at once hailed by the two men who had just called on him. It was a good job they beckoned to him since he wouldn't have recognized them, having only seen them in the dark. There were three seats at the table and they invited Jacob to sit in the empty chair.

The one who had done all the talking at the door, recognizable by his voice, held out his hand.

'My name's Lewis Denson and this is my partner Ward Kent,' he said.

Jacob did a double-take, but immediately tried not to show his surprise. The names were unpleasantly familiar.

Kent's name was on the seven of spades and Denson was spelt out on the jack. He couldn't avoid shaking hands with them. Then Jacob suddenly knew exactly who the silent Ward Kent was. This was not the first time he had seen those piercing pale-blue eyes, and Jacob knew it wouldn't be the last. Were they so untouchable that they could move freely in society without fear of being arrested? When they robbed the train they hadn't hidden their eyes or disguised their voices. It was Lewis Denson who had done the searching while Ward Kent held the bag.

Thank God he hadn't brought Rachel across to the saloon. But surely they must recognize Jacob? And who had the third man been, the one who had called Denson and Kent out of the carriage? Had Jacob now walked blindly and so easily into a simple trap? Yet he didn't feel in any immediate danger; it was too public for there to be any violence. Then he remembered that Denson hadn't hesitated to shoot the passenger in the foot.

Denson asked Jacob if he would like a whiskey. Jacob nodded and Denson went across to the bar. That was when Jacob saw the flash of silver as light glinted on the five-pointed star on Denson's lapel. So, that was why he was untouchable: he was one of the town's deputies. The corruption in Beckinson ran as deep as its river and Jacob had already gone beyond dipping his toes.

While Denson was getting the drinks Kent leant across the table and smiled unpleasantly at Jacob.

'Mr Martin is sorry he had to leave.'

'Oh?'

'Yes, he was hoping to meet you, but he was called away and asked us to give you his apologies. He's invited you out to his ranch.'

*I bet he has, thought Jacob, this is a carefully planned trap.* Whatever else he did, he decided he was neither going to drink very much whiskey nor go anywhere tonight except straight back to his own home.

'Anyway, he's left us to talk over the terms of business with you,' Kent continued.

'Terms of business? Mr Martin wants to open an account?'

'Yeah, that's one way of putting it.'

'Well, I'm sure we can offer him very favourable terms,' Jacob said. 'There'll be generous discounts for regular customers, and we'll be carrying all the latest styles from the East Coast and from Paris.'

'I'll let my pardner explain,' Kent said, as Denson came back with the drinks. 'Mr Burlen was wondering if Mr Martin wanted to open an account,' he said to Denson, and they both had a good laugh.

Lewis Denson held up his glass, he was clearly the more important of the two men, Kent was just a mouthpiece.

'To you, Mr Burlen, and the success of your business.'

They drank. Denson put his glass down carefully then looked Jacob in the eye.

'To come straight to the point, sonny, the terms are twenty-five per cent.'

'What?'

Kent enlightened him.

'Twenty-five per cent of takings. We collect once a month and late payments count as no payment, for which we take double the next month in addition to the regular payment.'

The quizzical furrow on Jacob's brow had turned to a frown of disbelief.

'It's a good joke,' he said boldly, 'but if you've brought me over here to play games, you should have said so and I'd have brought a deck of cards with me. As for your twenty-five per cent, you can tell Mr Martin if he wants to talk business he had better come and see me himself. And if that's the kind of business he wants to talk, he can go to the devil because I'm not interested.'

Jacob was aware that he had coloured up with indignation and had surprised himself with his plain talking.

'Very unwise, Mr Burlen, very unwise,' said Kent, shaking his head. Denson sucked in some air.

'Good to see a fighting spirit, sonny, but you've picked the wrong man to tangle with. Nobody here does business outside of Mr Martin's terms, but I'll pass on your message. Enjoy your drink.'

Denson and Kent got up from the table and left. They pushed through the batwings and Jacob heard their horses go off down the street. Too late now to do anything about it, what was said was said, and that was all there was to it.

Could it really be true that all the businesses in Beckinson were paying a percentage to stay trading? Jacob was beginning to feel that he would be doing the town a favour by taking a stand. But on his own? Only when enough people get together is there enough power for change. Or maybe when one person is sufficiently fired up with a score to settle, fired up with justified reason. Maybe. Maybe then things could change.

Sitting on his own with half a glass of whiskey to finish Jacob began to pick up snippets of conversation. There was the usual banter – which of the barmaids was prettier, which one was more likely to have a saucy chat, and which was more likely to allow someone to walk her home at the close of business. The price of grain and the price of beef cropped up amongst tittle-tattle about people's neighbours, and the usual gripes about wives were as thick as the tobacco smoke that hung about the ceiling.

The card tables were alternately deep in silence and loud with animation as games ebbed and flowed along with the chink of dollars and the expletives of the players. Jacob homed in on one table where the conversation between the calls and the bets was about the night-time shooting of a man called Pilotski. There hadn't yet been much talk of this in the town, which had surprised Jacob, but now he heard the players discussing the incident.

'. . . no way would lawmen come out here at night and kill him. What do you think, Jonah?'

'We all know he was a murdering villain but that don't mean he should be shot in bed. . . .'

'It weren't the sheriff here, or any of his boys, they wouldn't dare.'

'Not unless Mr Martin gave the order. He wouldn't. . . .'

'. . . perhaps Pilotski crossed him somehow. . . .'

'Vigilantes maybe, or bounty hunters?'

'Well I never did trust Pilotski, did a job with him once and he shot this woman stone-cold dead just because she wouldn't give him her necklace. . . .'

'I don't like it, whoever's behind it. . . .'

Jacob eyeballed the players and tried to mark their features in case he should come across them again. None of them sounded like very savoury characters. He downed the last drop of whiskey, got up from the table and went out through the batwings. He looked cautiously to the right and left, then, seeing nobody, he stepped out along the boardwalk. He had gone only a few yards when someone in the shadows grabbed his arm and pulled him into a dark alleyway.

'Don't worry, I ain't goin' to hit you or nuthin'. I jest want to warn you. I heard your conversation with Denson and Kent. Watch yer back; Martin won't lose any time in dealing with you. Maybe tonight.' The man disappeared into the shadows, leaving Jacob slightly shaken.

Jacob quickly made his way home and carefully bolted all the doors. Rachel, Anna and Ruan had gone to bed. Would something actually happen tonight? He crossed to the window and looked down on to the street. Barely a soul was to be seen. He checked the back window and all was quiet. But then he saw a figure darting quickly across the yard.

Jacob strained his eyes to see what was going on. Nothing, no movement, no sound. Maybe it had been a shadow. Perhaps he should go down and take a closer look.

Quietly he went down to the back door. He peered into the yard; there was no sign of movement but there was a light in the stable. Was someone in there interfering with the harness or the horses? Jacob slid the bolts and went out. Now he could hear the horses stamping noisily. Cautiously he crossed the yard to the stable, then suddenly he realized what was happening. Unmistakable sounds of crackling began to fill the air, smoke was drifting around and tongues of flickering flame filled the stable with a hideous orange glow.

Jacob roused Ruan and Anna before yanking open the stable door for the two horses to burst out into the yard. The bedding was well alight by now and with just two buckets and the yard pump to produce a steady flow of water, the three of them raked out the burning straw and threw buckets of water on to the boards. Rachel came running out, woken by the shouting, and was soon quieting the horses in the furthest part of the yard.

Now neighbours began to appear with buckets of water. Fire is not something you deal with on your own. With all the shops either joined or very close to each other, and the boardwalk extending all along Main Street, a fire is a shared hazard. Jacob and Rachel hadn't forgotten what had happened when they were living in Chicago in '71; it would take a lot less than that to wipe out Beckinson. Luckily, the Beckinson inhabitants acted quickly and a human chain of buckets soon extinguished the flames.

The strangest of ideas crossed Jacob's mind. Supposing the warning had actually been given by either Denson or Kent? After all, neither Martin nor Sandford would actually want the town burnt down. Healthy businesses paying a percentage into their coffers was what they wanted. That was why the fire had been started in the stable. That was where it would cause maximum panic and be least danger to other buildings.

Denson and Kent hadn't left the town at all. It was more likely that one of them had pulled Jacob into the alleyway and the other one had waited to set fire to the stable, maybe even waiting until he saw that Jacob was looking out of the window.

Luckily, no great damage was done. Neighbours went wearily back to their own homes, peace and quiet descended. The inside of the stable was charred but Jacob made sure it presented no further danger of flaring up. The horses were safe and, although slightly smoke-blackened and sweaty, the four human inhabitants of the property were also safe and sound.

'It wasn't my fault, Mr Burlen,' Ruan asserted. 'I never left a lamp alight in there.'

'No, Ruan, it wasn't your fault at all, it was mine. Anyway it's over now, so we can all go back to bed.'

'How did it start, Jacob?' Rachel asked.

'I must have left the lamp alight when I checked on the horses. I thought I'd put it out. Maybe one of the horses kicked it over. Anyway, it's finished, nothing more to do.'

Jacob got a quizzical look from Ruan who knew how careful Jacob was with lamps and the stable, but the lad said nothing. Back inside, Jacob reflected on the fortunate intervention of the stranger in the alleyway, without whose warning he might have come home and gone straight to bed. The stable would have burnt down before they had become aware of the fire, the horses might have been killed and, worse still, the fire could have spread through the entire property.

But that wasn't what they wanted, was it? What they wanted was to scare him into agreeing their terms of business.

It was evident that Mr Martin would not be ignored. Martin would get what he wanted. Well, Jacob thought, maybe he will, but one day he'll also get what he deserves.

'He'll have to do better than that,' Jacob muttered to himself getting ready for bed. 'I don't scare that easily. So, Mr Clem Martin, or sidekick Denson, let's see what else you're going to try.' He turned his head on the pillow, wondering what they might do next, but sleep got the upper hand.

# 10

The following morning Jacob was going through one of the catalogues with a customer when he was very surprised to see Lewis Denson walk into the shop as bold as brass. As bold as silver would be more appropriate, since the deputy was wearing his badge in a particularly visible way and making it clear he was on official business.

'Excuse me for one moment, ma'am,' Jacob said to the customer. Then, turning to the deputy, 'Mr Denson, good morning to you sir, how may I be of service?'

'I understand you had a fire on the premises last night.'

'Nothing serious,' Jacob replied. 'Nothing we couldn't handle with help from the neighbours. A simple accident.'

'Oh, I heard it was started deliberately. So I need to investigate the cause. If there's someone going round startin' fires the sheriff needs to know. He's mighty concerned about your business, you bein' new an' all.'

'Well, Deputy, that's real kind of the sheriff. Perhaps he'd like to look us up himself so I can tell him what happened. I don't think it was deliberate.'

'Well,' said Denson. 'Mr Martin wants to be sure everything is all right, him being particularly concerned about newcomers to Beckinson.'

Jacob smiled at the deputy.

'It's good to know so many people are concerned about

90

us. You, Mr Martin, the sheriff – a powerful group of people. My sister and I have been made to feel very welcome here in Beckinson and I'm sure our business will continue to grow. As you can see we have a pleasing number of customers.' He swept his hand in a wide gesture indicating the several ladies who were currently in the shop. 'Perhaps Mr Martin would like to bring his wife in too. . . ?'

'Mr Martin isn't married,' the deputy corrected at once.

'Well, nevertheless, I'd be pleased to make his acquaintance. Maybe we could open an account for him, for yourself too, perhaps?'

The deputy narrowed his eyes. He didn't like people who were too clever with words. Words tied people up worse than rope sometimes. But before he could say anything else Jacob continued:

'So you can assure the sheriff, and Mr Martin, that the fire was of no consequence. Nothing has changed. And I thank you most profusely for your timely warning, without which things might have turned out rather differently.'

This last comment was a direct remark aimed at Denson, a speculative shot in the dark about the alleyway encounter. But it hit the mark, Denson's eyes narrowed again and he turned to go.

'It was the first and the last warning you'll get,' he said under his breath.

'And good day to you, Deputy Denson,' Jacob called after him. 'Isn't it reassuring to know that the town is in such safe hands,' he said to the lady who had finally settled on a page in the catalogue.

'This is the one I would like,' she said to Jacob. 'Do you have any material with a similar pattern?'

Jacob pulled a bolt off the shelf and unrolled a yard and a half for the lady to examine.

'What would you say to this?'

At that moment Ret Murphy came into the store.

'I found these for you,' he said to Jacob. 'If you've got a moment.'

'I'll be right with you. Now, ma'am, if you'll excuse me one more moment, please do continue to peruse the shelf. And,' he indicated the senior shop girl, 'let Cherry here know if you'd like a closer look at any of the other fabrics.'

Jacob took Ret towards the back of the shop behind the cutting table where they could converse without being overheard.

'You've heard about the fire last night?'

Ret nodded. 'Yes. I was going to ask you if you wanted me to run a story.'

'Just a brief paragraph would do. Say something like: "A disaster was narrowly averted last night when a fire broke out in the Burlens' stable, but the quick action of Mr Burlen with the help of some neighbours," etcetera ... Something like that.'

'Consider it done.'

'Don't make a big thing out of it, just a bit of local news. Now, what did you find for me?'

Ret held out a small bundle of papers.

'I just ran back through some of the old boxes with the newspaper files. Amongst the old papers there were a lot of old Wanted posters, and in amongst them was a bundle labelled "for Mr S." I had a quick look and couldn't help noticing this one – Denson. Same name, isn't it, as one of Sheriff O'Donnel's deputies? Could be a coincidence.

'Now look, I don't want to get involved with this, so here you are, take them. And, please, I never gave them to you.'

Jacob took a quick look through the faded sheets of Wanted posters.

'Don't worry, Ret. I'll not tell anyone.'

'I'm pretty darn sure that box hadn't been opened for years, the clasp was rusted shut,' Ret said. He lowered his voice. 'And another thing, when we get the printing instruction, some of the names are wrong and some of the artist pictures don't match the faces. I have my suspicions that some 'wanted' men may live around here and I do know that recently a couple of posters were immediately taken down after going on display in the town. Sheriff O'Donnel himself gave orders for them to be removed.'

'You don't happen to remember who they were for?' Jacob asked hopefully.

'Look,' Ret said plainly, 'this could get a bit risky. I've got a wife, and a child on the way. I'd be mortified if I'd put them in danger. Would you tell me why you want this information?'

'Best not, you don't need to know,' Jacob said. 'Anyway, thanks for these, and if you do find any more. . . . Bring Mrs Murphy in to see us. Rachel would love to do a hat for her.'

Ret went out, raising his hand in acknowledgement. Jacob went back to the customer who was still trying to make up her mind about the material.

Late that afternoon, after the shop had closed, Jacob sat alone writing up the day's trading figures. In the drawer was the bundle of papers that Ret Murphy had given him. Now, with everyone else attending to other matters, he laid the posters out and gave each one the attention it deserved.

So, sometimes the faces were wrong and some of the names could be false, but even at first glance, when Ret had handed him the papers, one of the faces was a very good likeness, although the name was indeed wrong. There was little doubt whose face was staring out of that particular poster. Judging by the faded state of the paper and the thinness of the fold creases it had lain some several years in the *Clarion*'s files. Maybe it had never been pinned up in Beckinson, but there was no doubt that Ward Kent, falsely named as Ward Scott on the poster, was wanted for the murder of a young man in Denver. Maybe Ward Scott was his real name.

Either way it strengthened an idea that was growing in Jacob's mind about the men he was seeking. Just like the suit of spades on which the names were written all these men were connected by a single characteristic: not so much a black spade as a black heart. The path to criminality is short and steep. Maybe it started with taking a bribe to lie on oath and hang an innocent man, after which there was no turning back.

Jacob examined each poster carefully. It was possible that two or three more could be people about whom he would like some further information. But on another poster there was all the information he needed, even the name was right. It was the same name identified on the four of spades, Jonah Prewett.

Jacob paused a moment; something was in the back of his mind. He looked at the poster again. Yes. It was the same man, it had to be, it was one of the card players who had been discussing Pilotski's death – and not a bad likeness by the artist. It might have been five years ago, maybe some years more, but angle of the forehead and high hairline were the same. Other things can change, but the shape of the brow, if the artist gets it right, is a recognizable feature.

Prewett was wanted for murder and robbery. At a bank in Denver he'd taken a young woman hostage and she had accidentally been killed. Accidentally? Not really; Prewett had put her life in danger by taking her hostage. Why was he free to wander around Beckinson? Then Jacob remembered the card players saying that lawmen wouldn't come out here to kill Pilotski. Why not? Were outlaws untouchable in Beckinson? Jacob was still deep in thought when Rachel appeared at the bottom of the stairs.

'Still working?' she guessed as she started to cross the floor.

Jacob hadn't heard her approaching. He quickly folded

the posters and slid them into the drawer.

'Just finishing the ledger. I'll be up shortly.'

'Anna's about to serve the food and I just came to tell you it was time for dinner.'

'I'll come up now, then.'

He slipped his arm through Rachel's; his thoughts were not about dinner but about what he had decided to do afterwards. He suggested to Rachel that they should go across to the saloon and mix with the local people.

It was mid-evening when they pushed through the batwings into a room filled with cigar smoke and lively chatter. In the far corner a pianist was coaxing a tune from the piano and a fiddler was doing his best to keep up. The Burlens had barely entered when Jacob caught sight of someone beckoning to him. It was the land agent Dexter Gray, sitting with his wife and Mr and Mrs Tarne.

They went across to join them and were soon engaged in conversation. Barbara Gray and Amelia Tarne were already regular bespoke hat customers. Conversation soon moved to local politics as elections for the town mayor were not too far away. It was more than likely that Mr Ambrose Sandford would be returned unopposed for another term. Amelia Tarne was hoping her husband would be re-elected as deputy mayor.

Discussion about the town sheriff was a little more animated, Dexter Gray thought it was time for a change. Joining in occasionally with the conversation, Jacob was careful with his opinions. Listening rather than talking, he was paying more attention to the gaming tables, scrutinizing the facial features of each and every player. Bandits, robbers, murderers and such lowlife can never stay away from gambling, it's one of the traits that makes them criminals: the need for constant doses of excitement.

There were three poker games in progress and a noisy group at the faro table. Suddenly there was a bit of a commotion outside the saloon and four men barged in through the batwings, laughing and swaggering, all slightly the worse for drink. One, particularly loud and offensive, was holding a small piece of red and black material. He slapped his thigh and turning to his companions said very loudly,

'I told you she was a good 'un.' He waved the lacy garter aloft in full view. 'See?' he said, scandalizing many of the upright Beckinson citizens.

The barkeep called out to him.

'Jonah, there's ladies present. Show a bit of decency, for heaven's sake.'

It only served as encouragement, Jonah waved the garter like a little flag.

'But this is a bit of decency.' All four men laughed out loud.

'Jonah . . .' the barkeep repeated. But before he could add anything to his sentence the man had pulled his gun and fired off a round in the barkeep's direction. It clearly wasn't meant to hit him, but it punched a hole through a bottle, bringing down glass and amber liquid on to the barkeep's head.

The barkeep had ducked below the counter. He emerged, his hair plastered down with whiskey, which dripped off his nose and his chin. A few of the Beckinson citizens had taken cover under the tables at the sound of the gunshot. Slowly they too emerged. The man's three companions encouraged him to holster his gun just as Sheriff O'Donnel and Deputy Denson came into the saloon.

The sheriff cast his eye round the room and slowly took in the scene. It was obvious who had caused all the fuss as the four men were still laughing at their bit of fun. One of the local barmaids had come in with the sheriff and was standing behind him; she pointed to the culprit.

'See, Sheriff, Jonah Prewett, he's the one got my garter, and I want it back.' She stepped forward with her hands on her hips.

At the sound of that name Jacob suddenly became very interested in the group and watched with a keen curiosity.

'Now then boys,' said Sheriff O'Donnel, 'the lady wants it back.'

Jonah laughed. 'Well, what do you think, Ward? What about you Gel? Eh, Billy? Should she have it back? She shouldn't have gone and give it me in the first place, should she?'

'I didn't give it you, Jonah Prewett. Not if you was the last man standin' would I give it you.'

The remark was like a slap in the face for Prewett and he wiped his hand across his mouth before spitting on the floor.

'Well, well, pretty Polly, if you didn't want me to take it you should have kept your dress tight around your ankles.'

'Ease up, Jonah,' said one of his companions. 'You're going too far.'

Polly reddened; she suddenly leapt forward and slapped Prewett across the face.

'You damn liar, these three held me down while you pulled it off. . . .'

Sheriff O'Donnel held Polly back.

'Leave it at that,' he said, as much to Prewett as to Polly. Then, turning to the others, 'Gel, I'd thought better of you 'an that.'

'We ain't done nuthin',' averred the one called Billy.

There was a brief pause as everyone waited to see how the situation would play out. On the spur of the moment, Jacob stood up.

'Polly,' Jacob said in a quiet kind of voice. All heads in the saloon turned towards him. 'Why don't you come into the shop tomorrow; we'll be pleased to provide you with a new one. We've got a wide choice of embroidered ones with the most delicate stitching and. . . .'

'There you are,' said the sheriff to Polly. 'That's a kind offer, Mr Burlen. Jonah, you calm down. Billy, Ward and Gel, you three stay sober or you'll spend the night in with me.'

The tension eased, conversation resumed, the card games picked up where they left off, drinks flowed and food was served. Rachel smiled across the table at Jacob, realizing he had done a brave thing to intervene. But Jacob wondered if he'd been stupid, having already had words with Ward Kent, in the role of Clem Martin's mouthpiece.

'Well done, Jacob,' said Dexter Gray quietly. Randall Tarne nodded his head.

'You'll make a fine citizen, Mr Burlen. Beckinson needs more men like you.'

'Who exactly are they?' Jacob asked, sotto voce.

'Beckinson's untouchables,' replied Amelia Tarne.

'They all work for Mr Martin,' Randall explained. 'Ward Kent, Gel Redman and Billy Coats. Sidekicks, messengers. Above the law, it seems. The sheriff's always too easy on them. It's the unpleasant side of Beckinson.'

'Why doesn't someone do something about it? Call in a federal marshal perhaps?'

Tarne and Gray exchanged glances.

'We'd rather stay alive,' said Dexter.

Jacob decided it would be best to show no more curiosity; these men's names were well known to him, now he could match names and faces.

Prewett, Kent, Coats and Redman pulled out chairs at a card table and sat down. They ordered drinks from the bar and a deck of cards. Jacob noticed they were in that dangerous state between slightly sober and slightly drunk – a state when the slightest thing can spark a row. He knew Kent was on one of the posters Ret Murphy had given him, and Redman's high-pitched nasal voice was horribly familiar.

They were about to deal the first hand, but Prewett got up and approached Jacob. Up close he looked older, in his late forties perhaps. His eyes were slightly different colours and too close together, giving him a hoglike appearance, not improved by the scrappy remains of a couple of days' growth on his chin.

'Mr Burlen, the generous Mr Burlen, come and have a game of poker.'

Jacob shook his head. 'Thanks, but I'm afraid I don't play very well.'

'Neither do we!' Prewett laughed too loudly.

'All the same. . . .'

'No,' said Prewett, 'not all the same. We salute your generosity to Polly, now come and play, we insist.' He leant towards Jacob and the whiskey fumes were very unpleasant. 'Or are you refusing?' he said as his hand moved towards his gun.

Jacob knew it wasn't safe to refuse when someone who is slightly drunk and carrying a gun insists on something. He glanced at Rachel, then got up.

'Very well, just a couple of hands.'

# 11

With more than a small degree of anxiety, Jacob took his place at the card table, making five hands for the game.

'Good to meet you again, Burlen,' Ward Kent said, a twisted smile working its way across his lips.

'I bet you got lots of ladies' garters in your collection, eh Burlen?' said Gel Redman in his piercing voice: he was grinning lasciviously.

Jacob was anxious to keep the conversation at a decent level, knowing that they could be overheard by ladies' ears; he didn't want to offend any potential customers.

'We do carry quite a stock, he replied. 'Now, what rules and how much is the opening bet?' he asked, changing the subject.

'No special rules, just two in your hand and five up on the table. Ante is a dollar and every bet in dollars,' said Coats, taking charge of the gambling. 'Small change to a businessman like yourself. Customers in and out all day, we seen 'em. Making a pretty penny, aren't you?'

'Business is just getting going,' Jacob replied politely.

'Well, it's time to share some of your money,' said Kent as he dealt cards to each of the five players. 'If you're willing to give away your garters to a tramp like Polly, you won't mind sharing your dollars with four honest, hard-working men.'

Jacob ignored the remark, looked at his hand – the two of hearts and the four of clubs – and put in the ante. He knew that that was the kind of hand he should fold at once, but he pushed a dollar to stay in. Prewett followed with another dollar and then the deal continued with the betting until five cards were turned face up. They showed nothing to make Jacob's poor hand any better: it was one to chuck.

The serious betting then started. Jacob was keen to exhibit incompetence so that he could excuse himself from the game as quickly as possible.

'Here's two dollars to get us going,' he said.

'That's a raise,' said Coats.

Jacob shrugged to feign ignorance and two more rounds of betting continued before they all called.

'I'm not sure what I can make of this,' said Jacob, putting his hand down. 'There's a king on the table for me. But I can see you have three queens, Mr Redman.'

'Sure do,' said Redman, scooping the dollars off the table as his hand easily beat Jacob's as well as Prewett's pair of jacks and Kent's ace high. Coats had nothing to show.

'I'm not sure I should have bet with a hand like that,' Jacob said casually.

'Don't you worry 'bout it,' reassured Prewett. 'One good hand and you might clean us out.'

Jacob knew that was unlikely, and cleaning them out would be highly dangerous. He prayed that he wouldn't be dealt of pair of aces or get a high-scoring flush. He had to lose as little money as possible, but keep losing until he could decently quit. It was his turn to deal and he was careful to make it a clean one.

For half an hour the game continued – uncomfortably for Jacob, with Prewett's eyes on him, sizing him up. Worse than that, he could see Redman's lecherous eyes constantly focusing beyond the card table on to Rachel, and too frequently licking his lips. Coats never took his eyes off the cards, while Ward Kent seemed to be interested in nothing at all.

Jacob was watching Prewett. The more he looked at Prewett's eyes the more he saw the cold, callous meanness of a man who cared for nothing and no one. He played his hands with the same calculating coolness and to hell with everyone else. When Jacob saw him clumsily deal off the bottom of the deck, he knew he should have challenged the deal, but there was a risk that it had been done on purpose to see what Jacob would do. Wisely he let it go.

Jacob felt not the slightest compassion for any of them. They were no-goods, wasters, cheats, liars and no respecters of women, the kind of scum that washed up in every gambling den in every frontier town. That was all there was to it. But something about Redman's high-pitched nasal tone kept bothering Jacob. Had he heard it somewhere before?

At the end of the next round Jacob stood up.

'Well, gentlemen, that's me done for one night. Thank you for the game, it was a pleasure.' He left the table decisively, making sure they couldn't persuade or force him to continue. He rejoined Rachel and the others.

'How did you do?' asked Dexter Gray.

'Not very well,' Jacob replied. 'I'm a few dollars lighter than when I started the game. Quite a few actually.'

Randall Tarne leant across the table.

'I admire your good manners, Mr Burlen; there's no upright citizens in this town would touch a game of cards with those four miscreants,' he confided in a very low voice. 'Everyone knows they're a bad lot – the worst kind, in fact – but the sheriff is too weak to touch them, so we have to put up with them.'

'In my opinion O'Donnel doesn't want to arrest them,' Dexter Gray added, also in a very low voice. 'Why? Well he either takes a cut of what they steal and pillage or they're protected by someone higher up.'

'Who might that be?' Jacob asked in a whisper.

Gray shrugged. 'Your guess is as good as mine.'

'Sandford and Martin – do you mean them?'

'Sssh, keep your voice down,' interjected Tarne. 'I know I owe them some loyalty, being the manager of their bank, but they've got men in their pay all over the place. If one of them hears you say that, you'll be run out of town before you can count the fingers on one hand, and you'll likely have them all cut off as well.'

Dexter Gray took up the theme. 'They'll be nervous right now because of the shooting.'

'Shooting?' Jacob queried.

'That good-for-nothing Pilotski,' Gray replied. 'He was another one of Martin's men, a hired bandit. Someone took him out and that'll make them wary. Nobody has dared touch any of Martin's inner circle.'

'Long life to the brave soul who did it,' said Amelia Tarne. 'Those people are ruining this fine town.' She looked at her husband, knowing that they were in a difficult position: he owed his job to Sandford. 'If it wasn't for your position in the bank . . .' she began, but her husband raised a finger to his lips, to bid her keep quiet.

'We'll leave Beckinson when it's safe to do so. I can't just walk out,' he said. Dexter Gray joined in.

'We're all in the same boat; we owe our livelihoods to Sandford and Martin and they never let us forget it.'

'It's your choice,' Rachel said, in her innocence. 'You choose to stay, don't you?'

The two husbands and wives exchanged glances. Andrew Tarne spoke for them.

'Maybe, miss, but you be careful. You've made a good impression, people have warmed to you and have welcomed your high-class business. It adds a lot to the town, we want you to prosper and attract more trade.'

'Perhaps we'll be the start of Beckinson's bid for state capital,' Jacob said with a laugh.

'Sadly not while the likes of those four are allowed to roam free,' Gray said, discreetly indicating Prewett and his buddies.

'Well,' said Jacob with another hearty laugh, 'first off, perhaps we'll help clean the place up.'

They all laughed at that. Rachel turned to her brother.

'Jacob, I'd very much like another glass of the French wine which the barman has on the shelf behind him. Thankfully the bullet that man fired hit the bottle next to it, or I would have given him a slap myself.'

They all laughed again. Andrew Tarne stepped in; he took an order for drinks from their little group and walked to the bar. Half an hour later, after more conversation and when they had finished their drinks, Jacob and Rachel decided it was time to return home.

'That was a good evening,' Rachel said. 'Convivial company and two glasses of wine have given me a slightly light head. I'm off to bed.'

Jacob also retired to his room but not to go to bed. He opened the wardrobe doors. It was time to change his clothes. Bolstered by his belief that on the Day of Judgment his actions would be justified, Jacob slipped the Schofield into the inside pocket of his black velvet coat. Quietly he descended the stairs and let himself out of the back door.

The scene with Polly and the garter and their subsequent conversation had made Jacob realize that Sheriff O'Donnel would never arrest Prewett, or any of the others. Why was a murdering bank robber still free to walk the streets of Beckinson and abuse upright citizens with impunity? It was clear that Beckinson had two long-standing problems: the corruption of the law officers and the subjugation of the citizens by two powerful criminals, Sandford and Martin. It made his own place in the scheme of things seem quite unimportant, and yet he couldn't help feeling he had a part to play.

The names in the deck of cards connected a handful of men who symbolized everything that was wrong with the West, everything that prevented the Union's natural progress and prosperity. It was as if the tide of national economic advancement was sweeping across the continent from the civilized East to the Wild West and, along with pioneers and entrepreneurs, it was taking an unwanted flotsam of low and mean characters, fit for nothing but to be swept to the very edge of the land and eventually out to sea.

He crossed the yard in shadow, glad that a partial covering of cloud prevented the moon from shining like a beacon. Once outside the gate he set off down the back alleyways to wait behind the saloon.

It seemed an age before Jonah Prewett left the saloon, deep in slurred and noisy conversation with the high-pitched voice of Gel Redman. Jacob followed them at a discreet distance. Eventually they came to a shack on the very edge of the town. Prewett and Redman went inside while Jacob sneaked into the cover of an outbuilding and sat on a sawbench. Suddenly he became aware of a horse close by, snorting in his ear. He calmed it with a few soothing words and silence returned.

Jacob was deep in thought. If he had been a smoking man he would have rolled a cigarette; instead he took out the Schofield and spun the chamber while pondering who had the right to take a life? Was Rachel right, Thou shalt not kill? Where was the guidance in the Good Book? An eye for an eye, or turn the other cheek?

A gentle breeze stirred the leaves in the aspens. A night bird flew out of the trees and a four-legged creature scuttled past the sawbench. Briefly the clouds across the moon broke and streaks of ghostly luminescence passed across the shack and the outhouse. Then darkness descended again; not the kind of darkness that makes it impossible to see, just difficult to distinguish shapes. Soon a lamp was lighted inside the shack, throwing patches of light through a window and on to the ground.

Jacob shifted his position and stood beside the window to try and catch the conversation, but he could only hear disjointed snatches. He gave up and went back to sit on the sawbench. All he could do was hope that Redman wouldn't stay too long; the task in front of him wasn't pleasant to dwell on and the more he thought about it the more his resolve wavered. Eventually the shack door opened and light flooded out.

'. . . we don't have to worry about Burlen. The boss has got it sorted. He'll be out of business by the end of the month.'

'I don't like the way the goddam sonofabitch stood up for that tramp Polly,' Prewett said.

'You gotta leave him alone, Jonah; let the boss take care of things. Mr Martin knows all about Burlen and his sister. Ain't she a little cracker? I'll get my hands on her one day, then see—'

'She's the one you saw on the train?'

Redman laughed. 'Sure thing, but I had to call the boys off just then. Denson had shot some guy in the foot and things were getting a bit hot; we had to go. I'll catch up with her soon, then the fun will begin.'

Redman laughed revoltingly and took his leave of Prewett. The door closed and Redman walked off towards town.

So, that was confirmed: Gel Redman had been the third robber on the train. It all began to fall into place. Jacob's ears were still ringing with the man's foul words about Rachel. It solved the mystery of why Redman's voice had sounded familiar. It was the voice he'd heard calling off Denson and Ward on the train. Redman was clearly higher up the ladder. It didn't matter for the moment: the card in Jacob's pocket was the four of spades and the name on it was Prewett.

He pulled the Schofield from his pocket and approached the door. If he went in now Prewett would be caught on the hop, probably thinking it was Redman coming back for something.

He banged on the door, not too heavily, and tried to imitate Redman's nasal voice.

'Jonah, Jonah,' he said.

The door opened and Jacob pushed in. He immediately pressed the barrel of the Schofield into the middle of Prewett's forehead, pushing him back into the room. Prewett's hands went up in a gesture of surrender. In a quick single movement Jacob leant forward and pulled Prewett's gun out of its holster and dropped it on the floor.

Prewett's eyes narrowed to no more than slits in his face.

'You sonofabitch.'

Jacob kept pressing the gun into Prewett's forehead until they reached the wall.

'Keep your hands up real high, Mr Prewett, and say your prayers. Your day of judgment has arrived and I hope God can forgive you, because I can't.'

'All over a goddam garter!'

'Nothing to do with a garter. Ten years ago your lies and the lies of the other eleven men sent an innocent man to the gallows.'

'*What?*' Prewett exclaimed in disbelief.

Jacob grabbed Prewett's right wrist and pressed his hand back against the wall; then, in a swift movement, he pushed the Schofield into the palm and fired a deafening shot.

'The hand you raised to swear the oath.'

The shock of the shot and the instant pain made Prewett buckle at the knees and he sank to the floor.

'You're a madman,' he screamed, clutching his hand to

stop the spurting blood.

'For the woman in the bank, for whatever else you've done and for my pa, may God forgive you.'

The second shot followed, quick and precise. Jacob slipped the four of spades into Prewett's pocket and went out of the door. He took the lamp round to the stable and saddled the horse. His heart was thumping but he remained in perfect control of his emotions as he secured the cinch with a steady hand.

Leaving the stable door open he rode the horse a couple of hundred yards beyond Prewett's fence and into the woods. There he dismounted, removed the saddle, threw it on the ground and slapped the horse's flank. It trotted off into the night. Jacob forced a smile to himself, knowing this would give the sheriff and his deputies something to puzzle over.

Back in his own room, Jacob hung up his coat, put two bullets into the empty chambers of the Schofield and slid it back into its holster. He opened a drawer and took out a photograph of his ma and pa on the day after their wedding. It was one of the few things John and Abigail had saved for him from the farm. It had been in the box of his pa's things with the parson's letter.

'That's seven down, Pa. The five in the churchyard, gun-fighters all of them according to the tombstones, and I've taken two more. Pilotski and Prewett, both murderers. Am I doing the right thing, Pa? Am I?'

# 12

Next morning the town was buzzing with news of Prewett's demise. It seems the body was discovered quite soon after Prewett's horse was found, without its saddle, wandering around in Beckinson. One of the deputies had ridden out to his shack and found Prewett stone-cold dead from two gunshots, one to the hand and one through the head. There was no sign of the horse's saddle. It was rumoured Prewett might have been shot in a robbery that had gone wrong. The thief had seemingly stolen his horse and, in his hurry, failing to secure the cinch, rider and saddle had been thrown off somewhere along the road.

Customers in the Burlens' shop were saying that the sheriff had been out to have a look at the scene, but no more information was yet to hand. Dexter Gray happened to be in the shop with his wife; he leant across to Jacob and said, in a low whisper, that someone had done the community a big favour and he hoped the perpetrator wouldn't be caught.

Just then Sheriff O'Donnel walked into the store.

'Mr Burlen,' the sheriff called loudly across the shop floor, 'I'm told you lost a pile of money to Jonah Prewett last night in a game of cards.' He strode across to the counter, his spurs ringing loudly, meant as an intimidating sign of his authority. 'Is that true?' he asked bluntly.

'It is, sir, but I hold no grudges for it,' Jacob replied calmly.

'You know he was shot last night?'

'I've heard the rumours.'

'Well, they're true. An' I found this on his body. A playing-card. Anything to do with your game of cards last night?'

'Absolutely not,' Jacob asserted indignantly.

'An odd coincidence that you also stepped in and faced him down over Polly's garter.'

'I simply tried to avoid a difficult scene for everyone in the saloon.'

'Did you think I couldn't handle it myself?' O'Donnel said, rather sharply.

'Not at all, Sheriff. I understand you keep a tight rein on everything in Beckinson,' Jacob replied ambiguously.

'I sure do, an' I've got my eye on you.'

'Oh?'

The sheriff nodded. 'Yes, I do. An' there's someone wants to see you in my office.'

There was a pause as the sheriff and Jacob looked at each other without speaking.

'He's very keen to meet you,' said the sheriff.

'Cherry,' Jacob called to the senior shop assistant, 'could you look after Mr and Mrs Gray here while I go with the sheriff for a moment.'

'Yes, sir, Mr Burlen, of course.'

Rachel had been listening and came across.

'Is everything all right, Sheriff?'

'Sure thing, miss,' he replied. 'Just borrowin' your brother for a while.'

'Not for too long, I hope; he's needed here.'

'Be as quick as we can, miss.'

Jacob walked along the street with the sheriff to his office. The sheriff opened the door and they went in. First person he saw was Deputy Lewis Denson standing behind the sheriff's desk. Then he saw another man, who was seated casually in an armchair. He was dressed smartly in a long black frock-coat with a moleskin collar and was pulling on a cigar. Standing behind him with his arms folded almost like a bodyguard was Gel Redman. Jacob was taken aback but he was careful not to show it. Was Daniel walking into the lion's den?

Without getting out his chair the man acknowledged Jacob with a slight nod of the head and a patronizing smile as he blew a cloud of pale-blue smoke into the air. His clothes were extremely fine but he couldn't hide the roughness of his pock-marked complexion that revealed the inner low-life character lurking behind the accoutrements of high-life success. A livid scar ran across his left cheek, adding to the air of unpleasantness which was further emphasized by the cold stare of his steely eyes.

The sheriff closed the door. The seated man said nothing. It was Lewis Denson who spoke.

'Mr Martin wanted you to explain why you turned down the offer of a good business deal,' Denson said, sitting himself on the edge of the sheriff's desk.

'I didn't turn down a good business deal,' Jacob replied boldly. 'I turned down a very bad deal.'

Clem Martin narrowed his eyes but said nothing.

'Well, luckily you're being given a second chance,' Deputy Lewis Denson continued. 'Mr Martin would like you to think it over carefully before you answer. Thirty per cent of takings is the price.'

'Does it go up each time I refuse?'

Denson looked at Clem Martin for some help with how he should answer. Martin simply remained impassive and silent, taking in every detail of how Jacob answered and how he carried himself. Jacob was very aware that he was being sized up by Martin. Sized up like cattle in the auction ring to see if it was worth a bid, or should be passed over.

'Yes, it does,' Denson affirmed.

'Then you might as well ask for one hundred per cent because you're just as likely to get that as anything else.'

A heavy silence filled the room.

'I'm here in Beckinson to do honest business with honest people and that's an end to it,' Jacob continued. 'I'm sorry the law here doesn't see things the same way. Now, if you'll excuse me, I have a store to run.' He turned his back and walked out.

Little eddies of dust swirled across Main Street. Crows cawed in their aerobatic delight, gathering high up to battle pockets of gusting turbulence. Beckinson was a lively town and many citizens were already engaged in the daily round of shopping and gossiping. Little did they know that the town itself had its metaphorical turbulence gathering overhead.

Jacob stood awhile, pondering on what the day might bring. Fearing some kind of reprisal for his bold refusal to meet the outrageous demand for a percentage of the takings, he was wondering what Clem Martin would now order his men to do. He would have to be vigilant. Last time, a small fire, perhaps next time there would be no warning and much more damage.

Any day now Jacob was expecting news from the depot in Denver that his autumn order from Chicago had arrived. He and Rachel were awaiting assorted materials, trimmings and, especially, some mother-of-pearl buttons. Rachel was needing more lace, silk ribbon, coloured feathers and papier-mâché fruit for the finishing touches to a new range of fancy hats.

Sales on both sides of the shop were satisfactory, prospects for the business were good and the stock they had brought to get themselves started was dwindling fast. The new delivery was important to keep creating customer interest, but it hadn't yet turned up.

Jacob didn't want to bother Rachel with the difficulties that were bound to follow his refusal to pay Clem Martin a percentage of the takings. Following this morning's meeting it was clear that there could be no recourse to the law, as O'Donnel and his deputies were demonstrably on Martin's payroll. Things were beginning to look quite dangerous.

It came, therefore, as quite a shock later that morning when the shop door opened and Mr Martin strolled in. He was not alone; posing daintily on his arm was none other than Polly. It could have been as if their conversation had never happened. Gel Redman was close behind as bodyguard. Jacob greeted them politely, ignoring Redman.

'Good day, Mr Martin, Miss Polly.'

Martin nodded his head in acknowledgement.

'Polly has come for the garter which, I understand, you promised to replace. She's feeling lost without it, and it was my . . . erm . . . her favourite.' He patted her thigh suggestively with his hand. 'If you get my meaning.'

'Indeed so,' said Jacob, forcing a smile at Polly while inwardly recollecting the thought of Prewett's unpleasant last moments. He slid a drawer out from the counter and placed it carefully on top. His hands were shaking. 'Perhaps you might find something to your liking?'

'You've heard about Prewett I suppose,' said Martin, 'and his unfortunate accident? Shot himself while cleaning his gun, it seems.'

'Oh dear,' replied Jacob, wringing his hands to steady his nerves, somehow sensing that Clem Martin knew that that wasn't how Prewett had died. Was he testing to see how Jacob reacted? Had he noticed Jacob's trembling hands? Martin's answer was measured.

'Guns are dangerous things; you can never be too careful.'

113

Polly cast her gaze over the selection of fine silk and lace garters, lifted one off the tray and showed it to Martin. Jacob's eye was following Redman as he slid across to the other side of the shop, where he was now trying to start a conversation with Rachel. His high-pitched, nasal voice carried across the shop.

'A fine mornin', miss,' Redman said to Rachel. 'Polly's choosing a new garter over there with Mr Martin. A good selection you got. I expect you like the shiny red silk ones too, a pretty girl like you. They allus look nice on a fresh pink thigh.' He was leaning too far over Rachel's counter and his breath smelled of old tobacco and whiskey fumes.

'I'll thank you not to lean across the counter, Mr Redman,' she replied, colour spreading across her cheeks. His leering smile was extremely distasteful.

'No offence meant, miss.' His eye roamed across Rachel's dress and slowly over her shapely bodice before glancing to the display of hats behind the counter. 'A fine sight.' he said, licking his lips.

Misunderstanding his drift, Rachel was keen to make a sale.

'Perhaps you have a young lady who needs a new hat?'

'Mebbe I do,' he drawled. 'Mebbe I don't. I'd buy one for you if you were my girl. What do you say to that?'

'I'm afraid I'm far too busy to think about that kind of thing,' Rachel replied diplomatically. 'We're just waiting on new stock from Denver, and I shall be even busier when that arrives.'

Polly had concluded her deliberations. Martin spoke to her very loudly.

'You'll let me see you wearing that tonight, Pol,' he said. 'An' I don't expect it to be holding anything up.' He called Redman over and the three of them left the shop. After a while Rachel went over to Jacob.

'What an odious man, that Redman is.'

'Yes,' replied Jacob, casually. 'Odious indeed, almost as unpleasant as Mr Martin.'

Outside the shop Martin slapped Polly on the rump. Polly smiled and shrugged her shoulders, then coquettishly she tilted her head and walked off. Redman turned to Martin.

'Boss, I've got an idea to speed up the bankruptcy of that shop and those two troublemakers. They'll either pay up or get out. Shame really, that young girl is a real looker.'

'Keep your hands off her, Gel. I don't want no complications of loyalty. Now listen, I'm meeting with Ambrose out at the mine this morning. Come out later and tell him your plan – an' it better be a good one. I don't care whether they pay up or get out, but one or the other will happen, and soon.' He turned away and walked across to the bank. Deep in thought, Redman kicked at the dust with his boot. A trip to Denver was shaping up in his mind.

After attending to some routine business at the bank Clem Martin mounted up for the twenty-mile ride out to his silver mine at Devil's Leap. First, however, he had another call to make. He hitched outside the undertaker's parlour and walked through to the back room. Amos Quaide was applying some final touches to the putty plug in Prewett's forehead. Martin's lip curled in distaste.

'Nasty,' he said.

'Strange,' replied Quaide, 'it's the second one like it in less than a week. Shot in the hand too, just like Pilotski. Close range, both of 'em.'

'An execution?'

'Sure looks like it.'

Martin sucked in some air. 'Well, they were both wanted men. There must be a bounty hunter lurking in town. You let me know if you hear anything. Got it?"

'Yes sir, but they ain't taken the bodies, so no reward for

a bounty hunter,' Quaide pointed out.

Martin's brow furrowed; he turned and left. He crossed the street to the sheriff's office and pushed in through the door. O'Donnel leapt to his feet.

'What's it all about, O'Donnel? Have we got an executioner in our midst? What's going on? Two men down, both shot at close range, hand and forehead. This ain't normal.'

'I'm working on it.'

'Work faster,' said Martin over his shoulder, already on his way. He slammed the door, crossed the street and mounted up.

'I don't like none of it,' he said to himself as he spurred his mount into a fast trot.

Three hours later he arrived at the mine camp. The wind was whistling through the pines and he pulled his collar more tightly round his neck. Smoke was rising from the fires around which small groups of men were taking a short break. An appetizing smell of stew wafted across the camp from the cookhouse. Martin went straight across to the office, ignoring the men's greetings, and slammed the door behind him.

Ambrose Sandford was smoking a cigar, mulling over a pile of papers and open ledgers, a glass of whiskey on the desk next to him. He didn't get up, or even stir; this was Martin's mine but Sandford was the undisputed boss and everyone, including Martin, deferred to him.

Martin crossed to a sideboard and poured himself a whiskey. He took a hurried gulp. The message he had to give Sandford would not go down well. It would be best to get it out in the open as quickly as possible.

'He won't pay.'

Sandford looked a little quizzical.

'Who won't?'

'Burlen.'

'What do you mean, he won't pay? Of course he'll pay, or

we'll run him out.'

'It ain't gonna be that easy. He's an awkward cuss. Defiant. I don't take to him at all.' Martin turned the glass round in his hand. He knew Sandford didn't like him to come with problems. Sandford already had a low opinion of him, and he knew that Sandford was gradually taking over every darned thing, including the mine. It wouldn't be long before Sandford & Martin's bank was just called Sandford's. And there had been no mention of a share for Martin in the new Sandford Palace Hotel project. But Martin didn't know how to stop his partner: his very unequal partner. He raised the other point.

'An' that's not all. Looks like we've got ourselves an executing *hombre* in town.'

'What?' queried Sandford, not taking too much notice.

'First Pilotski, now Prewett.'

Sandford took a swig of whiskey.

'What's that to us? Ain't none of our business. A couple of no-goods, what difference does that make?'

'I dunno, I just have a bad feeling. They were on our payroll. Both of them were part of the—'

'Shut yer mouth up. It's a coincidence, nothing more. A bounty hunter who got disturbed before he could take the body, that's all. Ain't nothin' to it.'

Martin dropped the subject. 'Anyways,' he said, 'what's to do about Burlen?'

Just then the door opened and Gel Redman strode into the office.

'Gentlemen,' he said grandly. 'I have a plan.'

'Were you listening at the door?' Sandford demanded,

'No sir,' Redman replied, 'certainly not. I was told to come and tell you about my plan.' He waited a moment, then cleared his throat.

'I got two idees. The Burlens are waiting for stock coming to Denver. Should be easy enough to check with the railroad, then me an' the boys can rob the train in our usual territory between Cheyenne and Denver. No stock. No sales. Bankrupt before the end of the month.'

Sandford stoked his chin.

'The stock's already been taken care of. I've got it held up at the Denver warehouse. An' the other plan?'

Redman was instantly deflated. He paused, disgruntled.

'Well, this is a bit different, a bit more extreme, sort of final.'

'Go on.'

'O'Donnel said he found playing-cards on the deceased men with their names on. We could write up a deck and hide it in the Burlens' shop. O'Donnel would arrest Jacob Burlen – not the young lady of course, she's far too—'

'Redman!' expostulated Martin.

'Yeah, well anyways,' Redman continued, 'if we could pin a couple murders on Burlen, mebbe the federal judge could be persuaded by a jury to hang him.'

Sandford and Martin exchanged glances. Redman wasn't sure what was going through their minds, being entirely unaware of the memories he had stirred up.

Sandford cleared his throat, took a piece of paper and started writing.

'Go to Denver, Gel. Take a wagon and one of the men if you want. Burlen's stock has been impounded at Quincey's warehouse. Give the foreman this release note and bring the wagon back here. Then Burlen can come out here to get it and see the sense of paying regular. Go on, get out.'

Redman took the note and left. There was a deafening silence in the office for a very long moment as Sandford and Martin fell deep into thought about juries and hangings. Not for many years had such ugly memories come back to trouble them.

'Gawd Almighty!' said Martin, shattering the febrile atmosphere. 'Is that the past come back to haunt us? What was Redman thinking?'

Sandford's mouth worked hard to rid itself of a bitter residue while trying to find some words that would somehow clear the air and his brain.

'Let's wait an' see. If there really is a killer in Beckinson we want to know who he is and what he's up to. It could all be coincidence. Burlen couldn't be doing it – why would he? So if we pin it on him the real killer gets away with it, and that could be dangerous for us. What's your idea?'

In that very moment an idea did come to Martin. Supposing it was Sandford behind the killings – and suppose Sandford was planning to plant a slug to finish him too – and take over the mine and everything else? What if it was Sandford who had the deck of cards, and his name: Clem Martin, was on one of the cards?

He'd never felt the need to watch his back, but there was a nasty familiarity about the current turn of events. Martin was beginning to feel that there was no one he could trust. It was very uncomfortable.

Uncomfortable too for Sandford, having his own dark thoughts about the killings. In the back of his mind he knew there had to be a connection between the cards and the killings of Pilotski and Prewett but as yet he couldn't figure what it might be, or whether Martin could be somehow involved.

Both men realized simultaneously that they could trust nobody, and especially not each other.

# 13

Crossing the yard to the bunkhouses, Redman had no inkling of the muddy water he had stirred up. His priority was to get Ward Kent for the trip to Denver and the opportunity of a rowdy time. Inside the bunkhouse three miners were sitting at a table playing cards.

'Busy? Where's Kent?' Redman asked.

'Dunno, went into town, got a date at Sandford's Hotel tonight, going to have him some fun,' said one of the players.

'Fun? Listen, I've got a job for one of you.'

'We're due back in the mine later.'

'Oh,' said Redman. 'Sandford wants me to take a wagon into Denver. I need someone to ride shotgun.'

They all laughed at the ridiculous idea of Redman needing protection.

'OK,' he said. 'I'll wait for Ward to come back, or mebbe I'll go on my own tomorrow morning. Now deal me in, boys, I need to win me some money for a shindig in Denver.'

Redman wanted to take Kent with him for some roistering in the city; he wouldn't have been so relaxed about it if he'd known what Kent was up to in Beckinson.

On hearing about Prewett's death Kent had figured that Polly might need some comforting and he planned to be the one whose arms she could fall into. He had ridden into town and put up at Sandford's Hotel, where anyone on Sandford's payroll could stay at any time, free of charge. Sandford's Hotel, like The Silver Dollar were just two of the many municipal and community buildings owned by the town's Mr Big: Mayor Ambrose Sandford.

Having decided to smarten himself up a bit, Kent strolled over to the barbershop where he took a hot bath and a shave. He was planning on a night to remember and thought he ought to take Polly a gift. A garter would be the perfect thing: maybe she'd let him slide it up her leg. His imagination began to work overtime. He opened the door of the Burlens' haberdashery store and strode up to the counter.

'Good afternoon, Mr Kent,' said Jacob.

'I'm looking for a gift for a lady,' said Kent, as nonchalantly as he could.

'Did you have something in mind? A fine pair of gloves perhaps?'

'Possible.' He jabbed his finger at the glass top of the counter. 'What's in that tray? Are they garters?'

Jacob was beginning to surmise what was going on. It was too much of a coincidence that Kent was buying a garter. He obviously didn't know that Polly had already been in earlier with Martin to claim the free one. So what was Kent planning? A startling idea was taking shape in Jacob's mind. When Kent had left the shop with his chosen garter Jacob watched him cross to Sandford's Hotel. Everyone knew the top floor was Sandford's and Martin's private playground and that was probably where Clem Martin and Polly would meet later that night. Was Kent intending to muscle in unwittingly? Jacob couldn't see Martin deferring to Kent under any circumstances and certainly not where a woman was involved. Such a scenario could play nicely into Jacob's hands.

Rachel turned in around ten o'clock that night. Anna had finished washing the dishes, Ruan had bedded down the horses and most Beckinson citizens were round their home fires or in the saloons. Jacob had a glass of wine in one hand and a broadsheet Wanted poster in the other. When Ward Kent had come into the shop that afternoon, bathed and shaved, he looked nothing like the image on the poster. Not a living soul would have linked the artist's impression of Ward Scott to Ward Kent, but it was all the same to Jacob whether he went by the name of Scott or of Kent. Fact was, he was one of the twelve who'd sent his pa to the gallows; fact was he'd robbed the train with Denson and Redman when Rachel had been abused; fact was that according to the poster he'd murdered a young miner. Now his past was about to catch up with him.

Jacob finished the wine, stowed the poster safely and went upstairs to change. Before leaving the house he slipped the seven of spades into his coat pocket; then he closed the door, crossed the yard and headed off towards the hotel.

Taking full advantage of the slow-moving shadows cast by lazy clouds rolling across the inky night sky, Jacob came to the back of Sandford's Hotel. He jumped up and grabbed the lowest rung of the suspended fire escape and pulled himself up on to the ladder. Quietly he ascended the zigzagging flights to the top floor and settled himself by the door, his heart thumping with nervous energy. More from habit than necessity he slipped the Schofield out of his pocket and checked the cylinder. He snapped it shut and spun it round without thinking. The noise seemed horribly loud but was lost on the wind whistling through the tops of the pines.

Prewett and Pilotski had meant nothing to Jacob, they were of no account. Neither was Kent but, however loathsome the man might be, Jacob once again questioned his role as the avenging angel. He was driven to complete his task to honour his ma and pa but, rather than getting easier, the job was in danger of dehumanizing him. He was beginning to see how gunfighters were made, how killing could become nothing more than a job.

A door slammed inside the building and the sudden noise jolted Jacob. Slowly he turned the handle of the fire-escape door and eased it ajar. Inside he could hear raised voices, easily loud enough to cover any creaking woodwork. Swiftly he went in and found himself in a small passageway devoid of furniture. His eyes being fully accustomed to the dark he had no difficulty in seeing a further door, outlined by candlelight coming from the other side. The argument was emanating from that room.

'So what exactly is your game, Kent?'

'Well, I jes' figured Pol might be lonesome so I drifted in to see if she needed some comfort – after Prewett being shot an' all.'

'What do you say, Polly?'

'That's how it is, Clem. There was a knock on the door and I thought it was you, like we arranged this morning. It was Ward instead.'

'So you invited him in anyway?'

Polly paused. 'I didn't mean no harm, Clem. I said straight I was expecting you and he was taking a risk in case you turned up. But he told me you weren't coming so I might as well make do with him.'

'That so, Kent?'

'Pretty much,' Kent replied. 'Aww, boss, c'mon, it was jes' a bit harmless fun. Jeez! What. . . ?'

There was a gunshot, a body fell to the floor, then silence.

'Oh my God! Clem, you've shot him!'

'Shut up and get hold of his legs.'

Jacob crept to the door and heard dragging sounds. Suddenly he realized that they were heading for the passageway. He scooted into the darkest corner and crouched low. The door opened.

'We'll put him out here for now and I'll send the boys round to take him away.'

The lifeless body of Ward Kent was laid by the fire-escape door. Jacob's heart was in his mouth and the pounding in his ears was deafening. Discovery now would be the end of everything; even if he could pull the Schofield quickly enough he wouldn't be able to cock the hammer before Clem Martin drilled him. His mouth was suddenly as dry as a dusty street.

It seemed an age before Martin and Polly left the passageway. Jacob took a deep breath, then realized that what he had come to do had actually been done for him. All he had to do was leave. He moistened his lips. But there was just one thing missing, the hole in the hand. Could he risk a gunshot? In any case Kent was dead.

He listened for a while at the door but there were no voices or any other sounds. Martin and Polly must have gone down for a drink, Polly would certainly be shaken up. He squeezed the doorknob and turned it slowly, peered into the room. There was nobody there. He lifted Kent's body under the shoulders, noticing that the bullet had passed straight through his chest leaving close-range black powder marks on the shirt.

He dragged the corpse back into the sumptuous boudoir. He arranged the body on the floor, took the seven of spades from his pocket and placed it on Kent's chest. He pulled the right hand free and pressed the Schofield's barrel into the palm. Then, after covering the gun with a cushion to muffle the noise, he fired a single shot.

Quickly going back down the fire escape, Jacob leapt the last six feet to the ground and disappeared amongst the tall night-black pines.

*

Jacob woke late the next morning. The household was already in full swing. He could hear Anna and Rachel talking downstairs. The horses were stamping in the yard. He let one foot dangle out of the bed, testing the temperature of the air and deciding whether he should get up. He ran his hand across his face and felt the stubble. Today he would let the barber give him a decent shave; he always managed to miss bits round his neck when he did it himself.

Lazily he slid from under the covers, stretched and yawned. He took the stairs cautiously, poured himself some coffee from the pot on the stove and went down into the shop. It was eight o'clock and Rachel was already attending to a window display.

'I'm going across for a shave, then I'll be riding out. Can you manage on your own, just you and the girls?'

'Of course,' was the rather curt reply. 'We're quite capable of running the shop without you, Jacob. You men think the world comes to a stop when you're not in charge.' She smiled and shook her head at him.

He was a little embarrassed for having patronized her. Rachel's side of the shop was doing very well, her creations were much in demand. He withdrew gracefully and closed the door behind him.

Two men were being shaved in the barber's so he sat to wait his turn.

'Mornin', Burlen,' said Whiskers Campbell, the barber surgeon. 'Heard the news?'

'What news?'

'Another murder. With a playing-card.' Campbell paused between each short statement as his scissors opened and closed. It could take several minutes to get the whole story. 'This time looks like Sandford or Martin had somethin' to do with it.' Snip, snip. 'Top floor of Sandford's Hotel.' Snip. 'And we know that's their private apartment.' Snip . . . snip, snip. 'Victim's Ward Kent.' Campbell paused a long while, the scissors at rest while he puzzled. 'Shot through the heart.' Snip, snip. 'And the hand, just like the others.'

'Worrying times,' Jacob said, not displaying much interest. 'I'd heard these men were wanted for crimes of one sort or another. Pilotski and Prewett, Kent too perhaps. Must be a bounty hunter.'

'Can't be,' said one of the customers. 'They ain't takin' the bodies nor the hands, just shooting a hole in them. This ain't no town for bounty hunters. No sir, these are executions. I guess Sandford'll be behind it somewhere.'

'You'd better mind your mouth, Neb,' Campbell admonished. 'If they hear you talkin' like that you'll be next.'

'Tosh!' replied Neb, spitting some shaving soap out of his mouth. 'Nuthin' happens in this town without Sandford or Martin's behind it somewhere. This used to be a decent place but since they took over everybody has to watch what they say. I guess there ain't nobody in this town isn't in hock up to their eyeballs with their damn bank.'

They all got to thinking about the bank and their own debts, and that put a gloomy stop to conversation. Feeling as fresh as a new-shorn lamb, Jacob left Campbell's gossip shop, both delighted that the mystery was deepening and anxious lest anything might trace things back to him. The worst thing was not having anyone to confide in, not being able to share his burden with anyone – and especially not with Rachel.

Sheriff Hart's widow would know what was happening if she heard the stories. It was time he took another trip to see her. There was one card in the suit of spades – the queen – with a name that was both shocking and puzzling, and Jacob wanted to know about it.

It was late in the afternoon when he arrived in Crossing Point and hitched to the fence outside Widow Hart's house. She'd made an apple pie earlier in the day and Jacob willingly accepted a large slice with a cup of hot coffee. It satisfied his appetite and gave him time to pluck up the courage to say what he was thinking. At length he put the spoon down and drew a deep breath.

'Do you remember giving me that deck of cards? Well, all those names were hidden on the suit of spades. But I've been puzzling, Mrs Hart; there's a card that I can't figger, the queen. The name on the card is Hart.'

'And who do you think that might be?' She clasped a hand to her chest as if she had felt a sudden pain. 'Are you thinking it might be me?'

'No, of course not, ma'am, but . . .'

She fixed him squarely in the eye, and Jacob was arrested in mid-sentence. She heaved a huge sigh.

'Well then, it'll surprise you to know that, in a kinda way, it is me.'

'You?'

'Not direct, you understand.' She got up from her chair and took the plate from Jacob. She crossed to the sink and, with her back to him, said, 'It's Hal.'

'Your husband?'

'Yes. He was one of the jurors. Couldn't get out of it; they forced him to sit through the trial, forced him to swear the oath. He feigned illness and asked Judge Chainey to be excused but Sandford fixed that.' There was a long pause, then she turned round to face Jacob.

'You see, they were holding me hostage while the trial was on. Nobody knew that at the time, and I never have told no one until now. They told Hal if he wanted to see me again he'd agree to a guilty verdict. So he did. He carried the shame of it to his grave. The night before the judgement he deliberately swallowed some black powder. He was so ill they had to carry him out before the sentencing. Didn't make no difference to the outcome.' She sat down again in the chair and rocked it slowly backwards and forwards.

'He always said I was his queen. Probably accounts for it.'
A tear escaped from her eye and her lip trembled. 'That
oath was the only dishonest thing he ever done. God forgive
him, he was such a good lawman and a devoted husband.'

'I'm sorry to bring all this unhappiness back and distress
you, ma'am.'

'Don't you worry 'bout it, young man. I just wish
someone would put it right and clear Hal's name. You sure
you're ain't no lawman?'

'Quite sure, ma'am.'

'You look honest, though, and nobody ever asked me
about that hanging, until you. So, I'm going to tell you
sumpin' I never told anyone before.' She poured another
cup of coffee and gave it to Jacob.

'Well, nobody can touch him now. You see, Hal took care
of some of those jurymen. He never did nothin' dishonest,
nor outside the law, but he kept all those names in his head,
and when one of them was wanted for a serious crime, he
managed to shoot them dead for resisting arrest. Four or
five of them I think. Buried in the church they were.

'He always said they deserved to die for being murderers
by association. Paid to lie; guilty, all of them. Hal always
called them 'perjurymen', never jurymen. He thought it
might make some amends for lying himself. I think he
meant to get them all eventually. Guess they cottoned on to
what he was doing.'

'I can see your husband was a decent man. They knew he
hadn't got a choice but to comply. His name'll be cleared
one day, I'm sure of it. Do you mind if I ask one more question?'

'One more makes no difference.'

'Where did they hide you?'

'Took me in the middle of the night to Clem Martin's
mine. They dragged me into a disused mineshaft behind
the office in the main yard. Told me I wouldn't see the light

of day unless Hal followed their instructions. I was petrified. Hal always said it was either Martin who shot his own brother, or Sandford did it. That was the root of it all. Greed. All a long time ago. Now, if you don't mind, I need a nap. See yourself out.'

Jacob got up. 'Thank you, ma'am. God bless you.'

A smile crept across her face as her eyes closed. She was asleep before Jacob had reached the door.

Daylight was fading; it would be a long ride in the dark but the road was easy to follow and no doubt the summer moon would be bright enough to light the way.

Jacob eventually arrived at the yard with the moon past its zenith. Ruan heard the horse and emerged, bleary-eyed with slumber. Jacob slid down and handed over to the lad. He was glad to open the back door and climb the two flights of stairs to his room. He pulled his boots off and before he could do much else he fell on to the bed and was fast asleep in no time.

# 14

The following day Jacob busied himself in the shop. He was becoming increasingly anxious about the low level of the stock and the apparent delay in supplies from Chicago. It was quite a while since the order had been wired to Clifford; perhaps he should go to Denver and make some enquiries. He talked it over with Rachel that evening and decided it would be the best thing to do.

Early the next day Jacob stepped out into the sharp summer air. Ruan had saddled his mount and was just tightening the cinch. Jacob checked his gun; nobody in their right mind travelled the road to Denver unprepared for surprise encounters with wolves or even bears, and daylight robberies were not unknown. As Jacob clicked the cylinder, checking each chamber, Anna came out with a small package of food.

'I hope you won't be needing that,' she said pointing at the revolver. Jacob levelled the gun and pretended to fire.

'That's another one down,' he joked.

'Another one?' she queried.

'Wolves, bears, coyotes, you never know what.'

He swung up into the saddle and looking up saw Rachel standing at the window in her Chinese-silk dressing gown. He waved and she blew him a kiss. Ruan opened the gate and Jacob rode out.

'Look after the women!' he shouted over his shoulder to Ruan.

There were no wolves, bears, coyotes or any other kind of troublesome predator on the road that evening. He arrived in the outskirts of Denver as the night sky was turning from purple to black. He called at a livery stable first, then checked into Gray's Hotel, then went over the road for a prime rib in a noisy saloon. The day's riding had taken its toll and he was soon back to bed at Gray's.

After breakfasting on eggs and smoked bacon followed by hunks of bread and honey all washed down with strong hot coffee Jacob was apprehensive about the day ahead. He could already feel the exhilarating buzz of city life.

Settling here in Denver would have made much more sense than Beckinson. Trade was doing well in Beckinson but it couldn't compare with what they might already have achieved in Denver. Jacob had to remind himself why Beckinson was where he had to be, at least until this whole business was finished. Maybe then they could move into Denver. All that was for the future, right now he needed to track down his goods.

Quincey's warehouse was next to the railroad station. The crowded sidewalks and busy streets reminded him a little of Chicago, but only a little, as this was still a frontier town without any of the sophistication of the great cities of the East. But it was a busy and growing town. Fine brick buildings were under construction in every direction and grand residential areas were springing up for the burgeoning population. Once a ramshackle, cabin-clustered mining outpost, Denver was rapidly becoming the biggest metropolis between St Louis and San Francisco. Jacob tried to cover his face from the acrid smoke of smelting mixed with dust whipped up by the swirling wind.

By Denver standards, Quincey's warehouse was one of the more impressive buildings not directly associated with mining or banking. The bell fixed to the toprail jangled as Jacob opened the door into the main office. The reception area was busy with valises, people, crates, boxes and a number of uniformed staff wheeling laden trolleys. Jacob waited his turn in a short queue at the desk.

'My name's Jacob Burlen and I'm expecting a shipment of goods from Burlen's of Chicago. Do you have any information for me?'

'Burlen, Burlen,' said the clerk to himself, as he ran his finger down a list of clients. 'I can't see anything here. . . .' Then he stopped and furrowed his brow, 'Oh! Now look at that. Wait here, Mr Burlen, and I'll get a manager to have a word with you.'

Hoping for progress, the manager soon put Jacob right on that score.

'Come through into my office, Mr Burlen.' They both sat down. 'I presume you have a note of release with you?'

'A note of release?'

The manager blinked impatiently. 'To release the shipment.'

'What d'you mean, release?' Jacob demanded.

'We have a "hold until release" notice on the shipment. You must have asked us to keep it back until you wanted to collect it.'

'I did no such thing,' Jacob asserted, and a slightly heated discussion followed.

'Well, Mr Burlen, it would appear that this note, which has your name and signature on it, put a stop on delivery until you personally arranged for collection with a note of release.'

'When did you receive that note?'

'Let me see; it was a few weeks ago.'

Things were now becoming very clear. The fake note had been arranged in case Jacob refused to pay the local 'trading percentage' to Sandford. The entire venture was now at risk, Clifford's money would have been wasted and, much worse, Jacob would have lost Clifford's trust. So how was he to get his goods without Sandford or Martin knowing?

Just then the manager's door opened and the clerk came in, looking very flustered.

'Sir, there's a gentleman at the desk with a release note for Mr Burlen's goods. Having just met Mr Burlen I thought this was too much of a coincidence and I ought to tell you.'

Jacob got up and stood behind the window blind, he lifted a slat and peered through to the desk. Without much surprise he saw Gel Redman leaning casually on the counter.

'What shall I do?' the clerk asked the manager.

Jacob interrupted. 'I know him: he's a crook. Tell him to call back tomorrow morning. Say you're busy just now and would he mind waiting until tomorrow when the goods will be ready.'

The clerk looked to the manager and the manager nodded his approval. Jacob watched through the blind. Redman seemed to accept what the clerk was telling him with equanimity, and Jacob guessed he'd go and hit the saloons.

'Thank you,' Jacob said to the manager. 'They're trying to rob me. I am indeed Jacob Burlen Take a good look and wire Burlen's in Chicago, they'll give you a description.'

An idea began to take shape. It was imperative to find out where Redman was staying. Jacob hurriedly left the office and tailed Redman to a boarding house on the western edge of town. The Devil's Leap wagon was plainly visible in the yard. Jacob went back into town and purchased a deck of cards before returning to the boarding house and settling in a hayloft just opposite, from where he could observe the comings and goings. He whiled away the time playing with the cards, although that hadn't been the

133

reason for buying them.

Redman emerged at nearly five o'clock. Jacob gathered himself together and followed at a discreet distance. He was delighted to see Redman stroll into a noisy saloon. That would be the perfect place. Jacob followed him in and ordered a beer at the counter. Redman had wasted no time joining a card game and Jacob watched him laying out plenty of dollars, wondering where they had come from. After an hour of play it looked as if Redman was about to leave so, as he got up, Jacob walked across the floor on a deliberately intersecting route.

'Why, Mr Redman!' exclaimed Jacob advancing his hand. 'How good to meet you.'

Redman was startled, then suddenly looked sheepish.

'Mr Burlen! What brings you to Denver?' he queried, with a nervous rise to the question. Jacob smiled.

'We were only talking about you earlier, Rachel and I. Rachel was saying how very much she wanted to meet with you again.'

'Your sister's here too?'

'Yes, we're here on business; she's back in the hotel, dressing for dinner. Why don't you join us? No, that was presumptious. I'm sure you already have an engagement.'

'Not at all,' Redman said quickly, unable to disguise the curling leer of his lip. 'Just say where.'

'We're staying at the Grand Union, room 427; that's four flights of stairs or a rather slow lift. Say you come round about eight, let the concierge know and come on up. Rachel will be thrilled.'

'I'll do just that.'

They parted uneasily, as they certainly weren't friends, but both of them were inwardly feeling very satisfied with the arrangement. Redman's brain was already working on how to get the brother out of the way and give himself free access to his very pretty sister who actually wanted to meet with him.

At 7.30 Jacob had again taken up observation from the hayloft. Moments later the boarding house door opened and Redman stepped out. He had smartened himself up and was setting off at a jaunty pace. Jacob waited until he was well down the street, then crossed to the boarding house, went in through the front door and hit the bell on the desk.

'Good evening,' he said to the young woman who came in response. 'I'm looking for a room for tonight. Do you have any vacancies?'

The girl put the register on the desk and looked down the list.

Jacob's eyes darted over the page. 'Well, look here,' he said. 'Do I see Mr Gel Redman there, room 6? That's my friend. Would you call him up for me?'

The girl looked up lazily. 'I think he just went out.'

'Well darn that! My name's Ward Kent – he'll be mighty pleased to see me. Can I have room 5, next to his?'

The girl turned the register for him to sign. He wrote Ward Kent in the space, then took the deck of playing-cards from his pocket He pulled out the eight of spades and wrote Gel Redman across the top.

'Please give him this when he comes in. He'll be amazed.'

The girl put the card in the drawer and took down a key. She led the way up the stairs and unlocked the door.

'This is room 5, sir.'

Jacob made himself at home. He lit no lamps but drew the heavy drapes and sat in the dark.

It was possible that at about the same time Gel Redman was just discovering that no guests by the name of Burlen were checked into the Grand Union hotel. The chances were that he would be quite furious about the trick and would probably get totally drunk in one or more of

Denver's disreputable drinking holes before returning to the lodgings in a foul and dangerous mood. All Jacob had to do was sit quite still with the Schofield resting in his lap and his nerve holding steady.

Bored but alert, Jacob struck a match near the face of his pocket watch and saw that it was only an hour off midnight. What would Redman do when he got back? If the girl gave him the card and said that Ward Kent was waiting for him in the room next to his, he'd be up the stairs three at a time.

Then it suddenly occurred to Jacob that his elaborate plan might misfire, that Redman might smell a rat, become suspicious. What if he knew Kent was already dead? The subterfuge with the card now seemed like a foolish idea, for it might have given Redman a warning. What if he came into the room with his gun drawn, ready to shoot? If Jacob stayed in the dark he couldn't guarantee having the first shot, or its accuracy.

Suddenly everything seemed unnecessarily dangerous. Hurriedly he lit the table oil lamp. He was about to rethink the whole scheme when he heard the boarding house door open and close. Then voices downstairs, the unmistakable nasal drawl of Gel Redman talking to the girl at reception. Straining his ears, Jacob heard the girl open the drawer: the silence that followed suggested that Redman was puzzling over the card.

'Ward gave you this?' Jacob heard him say, slightly slurred but not totally drunk.

'Yes, sir, said you'd be mighty pleased to see him. He's in room 5 next to yours.'

'Is he here now?'

'Guess so,' said the girl. 'Never heard him go out.'

Footsteps on the creaking stairs, not hurried, not three at a time, nor slow and suspicious either, just ordinary. Then a knock on the door.

'Ward, is that you in there?'

Jacob simply said, 'Come in, Gel,' as brightly as possible, hoping not to sound like himself. The door opened and Redman entered the dimly lit room. He closed the door.

'Ward?'

Jacob stepped out from behind the heavy crimson drapes, the Schofield aimed squarely at Redman's forehead.

'Slowly put your hands on your head, Mr Redman.'

'Where's Kent?'

'Waiting for you,' Jacob said, cryptically. 'But not here. Never was here, nor was Rachel, you lecherous vermin.'

Redman sneered. 'You made me look silly at the Grand Union, I ain't forgivin' you for that.'

'That's nothing compared with what I'm not forgiving you for. You don't know who I am, do you? Or why you're holding a card with your name on it? You're just another one of the guilty rats with a long list of crimes to your name. Does the name Zachary Peterson mean anything to you? When you swore an oath and perjured yourself along with the others, to hang an innocent man.'

'Hell, that was nothing!' Redman said dismissively; then as the gravity of his situation began to dawn on him, 'I had no choice.'

'We all have a choice. May God forgive you.'

Those were the last words Gel Redman heard in this world as the room filled with a tremendous noise and a vast cloud of gunsmoke. The bullet drilled a neat hole in his forehead and threw him violently back against the blood-spattered door. A second shot followed the first in quick succession as Jacob placed the gun against Redman's right palm and unloaded a second chamber. The eight of spades lay close by on the floor where it had fallen out of Redman's hand.

Jacob picked it up and placed it on Redman's chest.

Distastefully, he bathed his wrist in blood from Redman's hand.

The two gunshots had brought guests crowding into the hallway. Jacob staggered out of the door holding his blood-ied wrist in a seeming show of injury.

'He pulled a gun on me and missed, but I didn't. Fetch a doctor quickly or he'll bleed to death.'

It had the desired effect. People swung into action to fetch water, bandages and to search for a doctor, not knowing that the body in the room was already a corpse. In the frenzy of activity Jacob slipped out of the house and melted into the Denver night.

Jacob woke very early the next morning to commandeer the Devil's Leap wagon and take his goods back to Beckinson. The sun was barely up and the air was chillingly cold. The streets of Denver were all but deserted. Smoke was drifting through the alleyways from the never-resting smelters and, in the strange quiet of this early hour, ingot-stamping in the finishing sheds provided an incongruous accompaniment to the dawn chorus.

Jacob was soon back outside the boarding house, won-dering how last night's scene had played out. Denver hadn't yet shaken off its reputation as a wild town and although the shooting would be reported to the authorities, it was unlikely that it would be investigated.

Even if the town lawmen became interested they wouldn't find anyone by the name of Ward Kent registered in any Denver hotel. Or if they did, it would be months before such news reached Beckinson, if at all. Jacob took a horse from the boarding house stable, a strong one with evidence of wearing heavy harness. As quietly as chains and traces would permit he assembled his transport and tethered his own horse behind the wagon. He drove slowly out of the yard and off towards Quincey's warehouse where the day shift was just beginning work.

Well before noon, all business accomplished, he was driving out of Denver. Towards evening he pulled up at John and Abigail's spread. With John's help, after a few words of explanation, they stowed the cart in one of John's barns. Pausing only briefly to consume a plate of bacon and beans with a hearty appetite from the day's drive, and giving John as much information as was necessary, Jacob mounted his own horse and rode home.

Deferring a long discussion with Rachel until the next day Jacob excused himself for an early night. The stresses and strains of the last couple of days had taken their toll and on hitting the sheets he fell immediately into a deep and dreamless sleep. This would turn out to be a blessing of sorts, otherwise he might have heard people breaking a window and entering the shop in the early hours.

Confrontation would have been disastrous.

As it was, the intruders moved swiftly and silently, knowing exactly what they were doing. When morning came Jacob would discover that they had left something very small and taken something much larger.

# 15

It was near eight o'clock when Jacob went down to the kitchen for hot water for a shave. Anna poured some into a jug, handed it to Jacob and then put some slices of bacon into the pan. He was tempted by the coffee pot gently steaming on the stove but he needed a shave first.

'Is Rachel in the shop already?' he asked Anna.

'No, sir,' she replied, 'I don't think she's up yet.'

'Oh,' he said, taking the jug back upstairs.

He soon came down again, smooth and refreshed. He poured himself some coffee and ate the eggs and bacon that Anna set before him. He wondered why Rachel wasn't around and asked Anna to go up and wake her gently. She left to do as he asked.

'Jacob! Jacob!' Anna called with a chilling urgency. 'Quickly!'

Jacob dropped his knife and fork and raced upstairs to Rachel's bedroom. He stood speechless in the doorway, trying to take in the scene. The covers were dishevelled, partly on the floor. Anna was standing beside the bed. She looked at Jacob.

'Where could she have gone?'

Jacob suddenly felt a sickness in the pit of his stomach. He could see her underclothes neatly folded on the chair, but a drawer was open and the contents in thorough disarray; the wardrobe door was also open and some items of clothing had clearly been carelessly removed. Rachel would never have left the room in this state. At the very least the disorder suggested a hurried disappearance, if not an actual abduction. Could somebody have already wired from Denver to Sandford or Martin about the disappearance of the goods, or about Redman? Surely not.

He put his hand gingerly inside the bed. The sheets were cold.

'Just leave everything as it is, Anna. I must get Sheriff O'Donnel.'

They both went downstairs; Jacob pulled out a chair for Anna.

'Sit yourself down and have some coffee,' he said. 'I'm sure there'll be a simple explanation. It doesn't look too good but . . .' he broke off. 'I'll be back shortly.'

'Finish your breakfast at least,' she said.

'Not now.'

He went down into the yard where Ruan was attending to the horses.

'Ruan, Rachel has gone missing, did you hear or see anything in the night?' He barely waited for Ruan to shake his head before making off for the sheriff's office.

O'Donnel was sitting on the bench outside his office door, smoking a cigarette. He raised his eyebrows in anticipation as Jacob ran across the street towards him.

'In a hurry, Mr Burlen?'

'Rachel's gone missing. Her bed's been slept in but she's disappeared and some of her clothes have been taken. I fear the worst.'

The sheriff leant back and lazily blew out a stream of smoke.

'Fear isn't a good thing, Mr Burlen. Maybe she's gone away for a while?'

'Impossible. She'd never go anywhere without telling me.'

'She's a grown woman, you know, and right pretty too. Perhaps she's eloped with a secret admirer. Maybe you're keeping too tight a rein on her.'

'Listen, O'Donnel, I've come here for your help and you're just making me out to look a fool.'

'No, Mr Burlen, not at all. I'm just sayin' things don't always look the same with another pair of eyes. You're thinking what you're thinking, and I might be seeing it quite different.'

Jacob stood silently in front of the sheriff for a moment, wondering what to say. 'The evidence, Sheriff, suggests she left in a hurry, just taking a few clothes and not much else.'

'Well, I have to say that's a typical scenario when a young woman elopes. Did you look for a note at all? They often leave a note, saying they're sorry and not to go looking for them.'

Jacob was beginning to doubt himself; could O'Donnel possibly be right? Sure he'd been wrapped up in his own secret life: his night-time tasks and then the worry of the undelivered stock. But wouldn't he have noticed if Rachel was getting interested in someone? Could he really have been so blind as not to notice that? He tackled O'Donnel directly.

'Why don't you come and see the evidence for yourself?'

'Leave everything as it is and I'll send Denson over when he shows up this morning.'

Jacob could see that there was no point in pressing his case more urgently, so he thanked the sheriff half-heartedly and went back home. Anna had cooked some more bacon and made fresh coffee. He sat down wearily at the table without saying anything. When he had finished he went downstairs to open the shop.

The assistants were already there and were busying

themselves with their own tasks. He called them together and broke the news of Rachel's disappearance. Then he put forward O'Donnel's proposition that Rachel might have eloped with a secret lover. He was glad to find that the idea was met with disbelief and derision.

About half an hour later Deputy Lewis Denson came into the shop. Jacob would have preferred to deal with O'Donnel rather than a known criminal masquerading as an honest lawman, but he took the deputy upstairs nevertheless. He didn't particularly want Denson to poke around amongst Rachel's clothes, so he closed the open drawers as soon as they entered the room. Denson looked at him suspiciously.

'So what are you hiding in there?'

'There's nothing that you need to see in there; just some of Rachel's personal . . . personal clothes.'

Denson ignored him and pulled the drawer open again. He put his hand in amongst the undergarments and then suddenly stopped.

'Ah-ha,' he said, somewhat triumphantly. 'What have we here?' He pulled out a deck of cards and looked at them.

Jacob was nonplussed.

'Well, what d'you know?' said Denson, showing Jacob some of the cards which clearly had names written on them. 'This is mighty interesting, Mr Burlen. There's been a number of murders, haven't there, with cards like these left on the bodies? I think you'd better come and explain this to the sheriff.'

When Jacob had recovered his composure he spoke.

'Look Denson,' he said, 'I don't know anything about those cards. Where's my sister? That's a far more important matter.'

'More important than murder?' queried Denson. 'Let's see what the sheriff thinks. Get going.'

Downstairs Jacob tried to revisualize the moment of

discovery. He was sure Denson hadn't put the cards in the drawer before apparently finding them, so they must have been in the drawer already. The only fact quite clear in his head as he was being marched across to the sheriff's office was that these were not his cards, but a planted deck. Whoever had taken Rachel had left the cards. Was this coincidence or had somebody started to piece things together?

It didn't take long for O'Donnel to reach his decision.

'The evidence against you, Mr Burlen, is powerful strong. I'm going to have to keep you here while I make further enquiries.'

'But what about Rachel?'

'Murder comes higher up my list of duties than elopement.'

Jacob shook his head. 'Sheriff, there is no way Rachel has eloped. She wasn't even—'

O'Donnel cut him short. 'I believe Gel Redman was pretty keen on her and by all accounts he hasn't been seen for a couple days. Sometimes you just have to accept things may be different from what you think.'

Jacob sank down on to the hard wooden bench in the cell. His head slumped forward. Of course Redman hadn't eloped with Rachel, Redman was dead in Denver, but Jacob couldn't say that, any more than he could produce his actual deck of cards to prove that the one in the sheriff's hand had been planted in Rachel's drawer by the kidnapper. The sheriff looked almost sympathetic as, shaking his head, he locked the cell door.

Jacob was trying to find the positives. Cherry, the senior shop assistant, would take care of the business for today, Anna would look after the house and Ruan would see to the horses as usual, but why had they kidnapped Rachel, what was to be gained? Sandford or Martin surely couldn't yet know about his trip to Denver and the recovered goods, or anything about Redman's disappearance. Had they taken

Rachel for the percentage money, and if so where to?

Then an obvious answer to that question came into his mind, but while he was locked up in the cell there was nothing he could do about rescuing her. Perhaps he should throw caution to the wind.

'O'Donnel,' he called out, 'can I speak to you alone for a moment?'

'What's on yer mind, Burlen?'

Jacob moved closer to the bars.

'Listen,' he whispered, 'I've got to trust you, O'Donnel. I think I know who's behind the kidnapping and where they've taken Rachel.'

'Yeah? And what about these cards you've been leaving with the bodies?'

'I swear those cards are nothing to do with me. They were left in Rachel's drawer by the kidnapper to throw suspicion on me. How did Denson know where to look? He opened only one drawer and put his hand right on them. That's why I wanted to speak to you alone. Denson's in on this. They're trying to get protection money out of me and I wouldn't pay.

'Now they've taken Rachel, and I bet she's being held out at the Devil's Leap mine. That's where they held Hal Hart's wife.'

'Hal Hart's wife?'

'Sheriff Hart. You know, while the trial of Zachary Peterson was on.'

'That was before I came here.'

'Exactly. They killed Hart because he knew too much about the trial.'

O'Donnel stroked his chin.

'And what has that got to do with it? Look here, Burlen, I don't buy any of this. Just cool off. There ain't nothin' I can do until I hear from Mr Martin.'

'You can't trust Martin!' Jacob hissed with alarm. Just

then Denson came through to the cells.

'What's he griping about?'

'Do you want to tell Denson or shall I?' O'Donnel asked. Then he turned to Denson. 'Something about a trial – Peterson or somebody – and Sheriff Hart being shot.'

Denson was silent, his eyes narrowed, he stared long and hard through the bars at Jacob.

'What do you know about it, Burlen?'

Jacob said nothing. He simply sank back on to the wooden bench and wished he hadn't opened his mouth. He had gambled a step too far.

O'Donnel and Denson left the cells and went through to the office. It was Denson who gave the orders.

'I'm goin' to ride out to Sandford; he'll want to hear about this. You stay put until I get back.'

Jacob heard him leave the office followed by the sound of hoofs galloping out of town.

'You see, O'Donnel,' Jacob shouted. 'You're just a puppet. Sheriff eh? In name only. It's Sandford and Martin and their cronies like Denson who rule this town.'

'You shut yer mouth, Burlen.' O'Donnel was rattled.

Just then the office door was opened and closed quietly.

'Raise 'em high, O'Donnel.'

The voice sounded familiar. Jacob could hear some movement but not much else. He strained his ears; the voice was calm, quiet.

'Move slowly, put your gun on the desk real slow. Now let's go to the cells.'

O'Donnel came round from the office, his hands above his head. Someone was behind him with a gun in his back. It was Ruan.

'Open the cell and get in with Jacob.'

'You're making a big mistake, son,' O'Donnel said over his shoulder. 'If I go in there you'll be guilty of detaining a law officer. You'll hang for it.'

Ruan cocked the belly-gun noisily.

'And if you don't I'll be guilty of murder, so move.'

Reluctantly O'Donnel opened the cell and went in. Jacob came out and locked the door.

'The horses are ready saddled in the yard,' Ruan said, poking the gun into his belt. Jacob turned to O'Donnel.

'This town needs cleaning up. If someone lets you out and you think you're the man to do it, choose sides carefully.' He put the keys on the desk.

They left the office and ran for their horses. Back at the shop Jacob rushed up to his room, grabbed his gunbelt, a couple boxes of shells and the last four spade cards. He called to Anna to close the gate after them and in the blink of an eye they were out of the yard.

'Where to?' Ruan asked, closely behind Jacob.

'John's ranch, then Devil's Leap,' Jacob called over his shoulder, and in moments they were galloping out of town.

They made all haste towards John and Abigail's ranch. John didn't take any persuading to saddle up and ride with them. He said he'd known the day would come and he was glad to be part of it. There was no time to be lost: the end of this ride was likely to be a concluding action and nothing was guaranteed to end well.

Galloping and cantering interspersed with recuperating trots consumed the miles, until a mile from the mine, Jacob reined in his horse, turned off through a tangle of scrub and pulled up. It was late afternoon and the sun was weakening. Big white clouds were high in the sky, lighter wisps drifted across in patches. The breeze sang in the upper branches of the pines while little gusts whipped up an occasional flurry of fallen leaves. They took the saddles off and let the horses munch the grass.

'We can't wait until dark,' Jacob said. 'There's a risk that O'Donnel will have been set free and he's sure to come out here real fast. Maybe with a posse. It was a mistake to leave the keys, I let my faith in human nature get the better of me.'

John shook his head.

'He won't find it easy to raise a posse. Most people know how corrupt the law is in the town and they don't want no part of it. They stay silent and get on with their lives, but they won't raise a finger to help O'Donnel – or any of them.'

Jacob was heartened by that.

'Well, we're three guns at least. But I hope it doesn't come to gunplay. I've a hunch they're keeping Rachel in an old mineshaft where they held Hal Hart's wife. It'll be risky but we've got to move in soon. What d'you know about the mine camp, John?'

'Not much. The boys are really wild when they come into town after payday, but I doubt they'll give us much trouble at the mine, unless there's a shoot-out.'

'Sandford and Martin are the ones I want. We must find out where they are – and Denson's out here somewhere.'

'Three against three,' said Ruan.

'And the rest of them; there's bound to be a guard with Rachel, and that's if we can find this old mineshaft.' The downturn in Jacob's voice told the other two he was losing confidence. John tried to perk him up.

'Do you have any idea about the location of the entrance.'

'Yes, I do,' said Jacob. 'Widow Hart said it's behind the main office; there's an old entrance in the rock face. I don't know if we can get to it without being seen.'

'There's only one way to find out,' said Ruan.

'Yes,' replied Jacob. 'Let's move out.'

By the time they reached the mine enclosure, the sun had lined the mountain peaks with a golden rim. Light would fade quickly and darkness would be a mixed blessing. They needed to move with haste and caution. They checked their weapons and crept forwards.

Devil's Leap mine property was marked with an ill-kept wooden boundary fence. This was easily broached and they continued their climb towards the main camp. As they came out on a small bluff the log buildings came into view, some fifty feet below their position. The main office was easy enough to spot, being away from the bunkhouses and well away from the crushing and stamping sheds which were stepped down the side of the hill, where gravity and water would play their part. A stream tumbled from high up on the top of the rock face, partly diverted to feed the crushing sheds.

'That's the Devil's Leap,' said John, pointing to the waterfall. 'It's the start of the river that winds through Beckinson. Local legend says Indians used to throw victims off the top of the cliff.'

'How did they get up there?' Jacob asked.

'No idea.'

Behind the main office building the rock face looked blank and forbidding. There was no clear sign of any disused mine entrance. John scanned with binoculars.

'Can't see too much that looks like an old entrance, although it's all well overgrown. There's a stack of old planks, that's all. I've got to get down there and scuff about.'

'Be careful,' said John. Jacob nodded.

'You two keep an eye out here, I'll go and scratch around a bit.'

Jacob left them and homed in on the stack of planks. Sure enough there were clear signs that the planks had been moved. Up close, Jacob could see they were covering a small grille. There was a chain and padlock. The lock was undone and the chain hung loosely around the bars. He moved one of the planks aside.

At that moment someone came out of the main office

carrying a tray with a plate of food. Ruan whistled a warning to Jacob but, in his haste to hide, Jacob knocked a plank to the ground with a thud. In a flash the man had dropped the tray and his gun was drawn. Jacob had no time to react. John and Ruan could only watch as Jacob raised his hands above his head and was forced round to the front of the office and inside.

'Hell!' said John. 'This has got a whole lot more difficult. Listen, that tray was likely going into the mineshaft. Rachel has to be in there. Ruan, you have to go down and see, this has to be our only chance while they quiz Jacob. I'll stay here on lookout.'

# 16

Ruan made a dash for the rock face. Quickly spotting the open lock, he grabbed the chain and padlock off the gate and hung it round his neck. Inside the shaft daylight quickly disappeared.

'Rachel! Rachel!' he called. 'Are you in here? It's me, Ruan.'

'Ruan? Yes, I'm here,' came the excited reply. 'Further in. Feel your way along the wall.'

The wall was slippery with water and the floor was very uneven. Some way into the darkness Ruan spotted a glimmer of light. His eyes gradually adjusted, and after he'd turned a couple of corners candlelight cast a dull glow on Rachel sitting on a rug, her hands tied behind her back. He cut the cords and lifted her to her feet.

'Thank goodness!' Rachel said. 'Where's Jacob?'

'He's outside,' Ruan replied, dissembling. 'We need to get you away first.'

'First?' Rachel queried, but Ruan made no reply as he hurried her across to where John was waiting.

'Where's Jacob?' she asked.

'It's not good news,' John replied. 'He's in there.' He said pointed to the log cabin. 'Somebody was bringing you some grub.'

'That'd be Billy Coats,' said Rachel. 'He's the one guarding me. He's nothing, just a weak sidekick.'

'Maybe,' said John. 'But he got Jacob nevertheless, and he's taken him inside.'

'There's a side door,' Rachel said. 'Round the other side from here. It goes into a small back office. It's where they took me first, before they hustled me out and into that black tunnel.'

John looked at Ruan.

'So maybe four in there, Coats and Denson for sure, and perhaps Martin and Sandford.'

'No,' Rachel corrected. 'When Billy Coats went to get me some food he said Clem Martin would be wanting to talk to me when he got back from the workings. And I doubt Sandford is here now; I heard them say he was going to Denver for something.'

This time Ruan looked at John. 'So, just two. Let's do it.'

'Wait,' said John. 'We don't get more'n one chance at this. Let's get Rachel to the horses first.'

'No, I'm staying here,' she said. 'I can warn you if anyone comes over to the office.'

John looked at her, nodded his head and gave her his Winchester.

'All right, Rachel. Just shoot into the air if anyone approaches while we're in there – and hold it steady or you'll break your arm.'

Without more ado John and Ruan made their way under cover as far as possible, then made a dash for the side door. They were out of sight of Rachel, who was scanning the compound for any movement.

Ruan put his ear to the door and listened. It seemed like good news. Apart from Jacob's there were only two other voices. It might be possible to rush them.

John had a better idea.

'Ruan,' he whispered, 'I'm going round to the front, I'll

152

knock on the office door. They won't be expecting me, so they'll be off their guard. With a bit of luck one of them will come through to see who it is. You can rush the back office after you hear me knocking, I'll draw immediately on whoever is in there an' you do the same through this door.'

Ruan nodded in agreement, licking his lips with nervous anticipation. John left him and hurried to the front of the office. Then it all happened so quickly nobody could tell the exact order of events.

John knocked on the office door and walked in, Lewis Denson came out of the back office: John had his gun levelled. Denson was taken completely by surprise and raised his hands. At the same time Ruan had burst in through the side door, but Billy Coats already had his gun in his hand. Coats fired a wild shot towards the side door; Ruan fired twice, making Jacob throw himself on the floor. The noise and the smoke were deafening, blinding and confusing. Coats was groaning.

Now Jacob saw his chance. He got to his feet, grabbed his gun from the table and put an end to Coats's suffering with a bullet in the chest. Through the open door Jacob could see Denson with his hands held high and John close behind. Jacob told Denson to come into the back office.

'Sit in the chair, Denson. Ruan, tie his hands to the chair. This man is a kidnapper, a train robber, masquerading as a lawman. And he tried to frame me with a deck of cards. What do you say to that, Denson?' There was no reply. Jacob turned to John. 'Is Rachel safe?'

'Yes, she's keeping watch some ways off. Thought Clem Martin was going to see her later and she thinks Sandford's gone to Denver.'

Jacob turned back to Denson.

'Where's Martin?' There was no reply so Jacob struck him across the cheek with the barrel of his gun. 'Where's Martin?'

153

Denson lifted his head, a trickle of blood ran from the corner of his mouth.

'That's enough.' He coughed. 'Went to the workings, said he was going to have some fun with your sister later this evening.'

Jacob spoke to John. 'Since nobody's come to investigate the shooting, take Ruan and Rachel back into town. I'm staying here for a while. There's more to finish. If you run into O'Donnel see which side he's chosen.'

When they had gone Jacob sat on a chair in front of Denson. He held his gun in his lap.

'Whose idea was the kidnapping and the fake deck of cards?'

There was a long pause. Jacob could see Denson's tongue moving around in his mouth. It was feeling for the damage already done and wondering what to say to avoid another blow. Jacob held his gun near Denson's jaw. Denson decided to speak.

'Redman's idea for the kidnap. He wanted to—'

'Yes, I know what he wanted, and he's already paid the price for that and a lot more besides. And the cards?'

'Sandford. He said it would get you into jail and your business would collapse. You should've paid the percentage. Sandford wouldn't stand for you not paying. Said you'd be trouble. Wanted you out of town.' He paused, then went on.

'Listen, mister,' Denson pleaded, 'we just do as we're told. Sandford and Martin run the town and everything in it, including the law.'

'The law,' Jacob repeated. 'Oh yes, the law that hanged an innocent man. This is nothing to do with percentages. This is about murder. You played your part in that, didn't you?'

'Me? What d'yer mean?'

'You sent Zachary Peterson to the gallows for a murder

he didn't commit.'

'Peterson? Geez! That was an age ago.'

'But you lied under oath, which makes you guilty of murdering my pa. I'm here for justice and to uphold the law.'

'Your pa?' Denson queried. Then, panic stricken, he desperately tried to break free of the bindings, but Jacob had already levelled his gun. He fired a single shot through Denson's forehead, throwing him and the chair against the wall. Then he calmly cut the cords and carried Denson's body out through the side door and into the old tunnel.

He returned a moment later and tidied up as best he could. He tried to wipe the blood away but had to give up on that. Next, he hoisted Coats's body over his shoulder and took him to the tunnel. He laid the two bodies side by side on the rug that Rachel had been sitting on. He arranged their right hands, palms upwards beside their heads, and shot a hole in each one. Then took two cards out of his pocket. The jack of spades was laid over the hole in Denson's palm and Coats got the three of spades.

There was nothing more to do now but wait for Martin to come for some fun with Rachel. He opened the Schofield's cylinder and filled the empty chambers. He moved away from the light of the candle, sat down and crossed his legs.

'We're nearly there, Pa. Still don't know if I'm right to do this. But they were all responsible for taking you and Ma – all twelve jurymen gone. Now just Sandford and Martin. I can forgive Hal Hart: he did try to make amends by getting rid of some of the others.'

Jacob spun the chamber of the Schofield nervously.

'If I die now, at least I tried to put things right for you, didn't I, Pa? Honour thy mother and father – God will forgive me, won't he?'

His musings were brought to an abrupt end as he heard voices and footsteps at the entrance to the tunnel.

Instinctively he drew further back, round more corners into the darkness.

'Listen, Clem, I think we got ourselves a problem.'

Straining his ears, which had suddenly begun to blood-throb with fear, Jacob knew it would only be a matter of time before they came into the shaft. They being, without doubt, Sandford and Martin. So Sandford hadn't gone to Denver. Luckily Jacob's eyes had become accustomed to the dark and, running his hand along the wall behind him, he crept further in. Looking ahead, he was surprised to make out the faintest glimmer of light high up, it was catching the edge of steps cut into the side of a natural shaft spiralling up towards daylight. This had never been a mineshaft; it was a way up to the waterfall. The quiet was suddenly shattered.

'Jesus Christ! Ambrose,' Clem shouted. 'What in hell have we got here?'

There was a short pause. Then Sandford said, accusingly.

'It's Denson and Coats, and more playing-cards. You knew about this, didn't you Clem. That's why you've brought me in here. Going to make it three, are you?'

Clem was almost squealing.

'What? This ain't nothin' to do with me, I swear, Ambrose . . . the girl was here. . . .'

'Really? An opportunity to finish me off too, and take back control of everything, eh? I always suspected you were behind the killings. It was just a matter of time. Well, you miscalculated, Clem.'

'No – no – look, Ambrose, this ain't—'

'Too late, Clem, I said we had a problem, and I guess this confirms it's you. Time to part ways. . . .'

The shaft was filled with an ear-splitting noise as a handgun was discharged. The dull groan and thud needed no guesswork as to what had happened. Jacob instantly tightened his grip on the Schofield and pulled back the hammer.

He was breathing hard. He took a deep breath to speak out loud.

'That leaves just one,' he said loudly out of the darkness.

'What? . . . Who's there?'

'An avenging angel,' Jacob said, hearing footsteps coming further into the shaft. 'Yes, keep on coming and see who it is.'

'Damn your eyes!'

A shot was fired; it ricocheted dangerously off the walls, zinging around in the dark. Jacob was retreating slowly up the rock-cut steps towards the speck of daylight. He was sure his pursuer wouldn't be able to see him in the darkness; shooting was pointless.

'That's both of them, isn't it?' Jacob goaded. 'First was Tod, all those years ago, and now Clem. I guess that'll give you control of the mine and the whole damn town.'

'Who are you?'

'I was there, Sandford. I was there, close by, when you shot Tod, and I'm here again, when you've just shot Clem. But it's not for them that you're going to die.'

Sandford was creeping along the wall, feeling his way in the dark.

'Listen, whoever you are, we can do a deal—'

Jacob was sure Sandford was on the steps too. He cut him short.

'We can. I've just got one more card to deal. An ace with two names, and one of them is yours.'

'But why? See sense, let's do a deal. What is it you want?'

Jacob was almost at the top of the steps, he could feel a wooden grille above his head. He pushed and it opened slightly into undergrowth. He eased himself out, squeezing through the grille. He could hear the water tumbling over the edge; he had come out at the top of the rock face by the Devil's Leap. Hurriedly he retreated away from the grille. Sandford's gun appeared first, then a shot was fired wildly into the air as Sandford himself leapt up from the shaft.

'Burlen!' he exclaimed.

The two men looked at each other, both with drawn guns, but one was aimed steadily at the other's forehead.

'Yes, Burlen. Or Peterson.'

Sandford's brow furrowed.

'Peterson?'

'Justice has at last caught up with you.'

At that moment there was a cacophony of noise as a posse of riders galloped into the yard, distracting the two men with their shouting and pointing at them so close to the edge.

'Don't do nuthin' silly,' O'Donnel shouted up at them. 'Put your guns away, both of you, and come down.'

There were about ten people below and a number of guns pointing upwards.

'What do you say to that, Burlen?' Sandford said, confident that he'd been saved by the posse. 'I told you we could do a deal. I'm still offerin'.'

Jacob's lip curled with derision. 'No deal.'

He fired a single shot and Sandford fell back, a clean hole drilled through his forehead. Jacob took the last card from his pocket, he cocked and fired once more, then laid the ace on Sandford's bloody palm. He looked down at the posse and raised his hands to show the shooting was over: he was giving himself up.

As soon as Jacob appeared down in the yard Rachel ran towards him and flung her arms round his neck. The group had swelled with mine workers who had come up to see what was going on. But there at the front Jacob saw John and Ruan, and also Dexter Gray and Randall Tarne amongst the posse.

O'Donnel came forward.

'You're a foolhardy young man,' he said, 'but brave too. Your sister told me everything I needed to know before riding out here. You're under arrest, of course, but it's up to the townsfolk where we go from here.'

'Don't worry about that,' said Randall Tarne, reassuringly. 'You've done a fine thing.'

It was a subdued party that wound its way back through the woods into Beckinson. News had travelled fast, of course, with the help of Ruan riding ahead, and townsfolk were already lining the boardwalks to welcome the party back. Jacob felt rather uncomfortable with the adulation and hats being thrown into the air, but his sister riding beside him couldn't help giving in to a feeling of pride.

Over the next few days the shop was busy beyond belief. Not just with customers but with well-wishers too. Ret Murphy was one of the first to pay his respects and said he was organizing a street party. He said it really did feel as if a great weight had been lifted off the shoulders of Beckinson and consequently he was planning a major poster campaign to attract tourists, and would Jacob be willing to write up his story, as Ret was sure it would pull in the punters, eager to meet the hero.

'And of course they're bound to visit your shop,' he added with a smile, raising his eyebrows.

Jacob wanted no publicity for himself, but he saw how a story about cleaning up the 'Wild West' could draw in tourists and that would be good for the town.

Ownership of the mine, the hotels and so many other things were taken over by the town council for the good of all the inhabitants. Randall Tarne was immediately appointed mayor, standing unopposed, and he'd asked Jacob if he'd like to run for deputy mayor. Jacob had felt very honoured but declined, saying he had a business to build first. However, there was a matter of a formal pardon which Jacob would like Mayor Tarne to action.

'Of course you'll be pardoned,' Randall Tarne said.

'I wasn't thinking about me,' Jacob replied.

There were two things Jacob had wanted to resolve. He had already visited Amos Quaide, the undertaker, and ordered a new headstone for his parents' grave. Then, the day before the street party Jacob told Anna to make up the spare-room for a guest. All their friends and acquaintances, along with the whole town, would be making merry, and Jacob wanted one more person to join the celebration. He asked Ruan to saddle his horse.

Rachel appeared in the yard.

'Anna says someone's coming to stay a couple of nights for the street party; is that right?'

'It certainly is,' Jacob replied, deliberately being evasive which he knew Rachel couldn't ignore. She rose to the bait.

'Might I ask who?'

'You might,' he said, 'but I'm not telling. Just a lady.'

'Oh, you dark horse, Jacob,' she said, arms akimbo. 'So that's what you've been up to, and I never guessed. Was it only John you met at the black tree?'

'I'll be bringing her back in a buggy.'

'Ooohh, will you?' she said, excitedly jumping to all the wrong conclusions, exactly as Jacob had hoped. 'Who is she?'

He smiled broadly to himself for the subterfuge and left the yard, trotting down Main Street. Fumbling in his pocket he checked for the official document with Mayor Tarne's signature and, still smiling to himself, galloped away down the road to Crossing Point.

# Warwickshire County Council

| | | | |
|---|---|---|---|
| Nov 7/18 | | | LiL |
| | | | |
| | | | |
| | | | |
| | | | |
| | | | |
| | | | |
| | | | |
| | | | |
| | | | |
| | | | |

This item is to be returned or renewed before the latest date above. It may be borrowed for a further period if not in demand. **To renew your books:**

- **Phone the 24/7 Renewal Line 01926 499273 or**
- **Visit www.warwickshire.gov.uk/libraries**

  **Discover ● Imagine● Learn ● *with libraries***

**Warwickshire**
County Council

Working for
Warwickshire

014232055 X